The Weaver of Worlds

Echoes of Solara

"This book is a work of fiction. While the character and their journey were inspired by the spirit and creativity of a real individuals, the story, characters, and events contained within are entirely products of imagination and are not based on real life. This narrative was created with the assistance of artificial intelligence."

By Richard Dell Schwarz

Forward

To my dearest Mia,

As I sit down to write this, I can't help but smile, thinking of all the adventures we've imagined together and the stories we've shared. This second book in *The Weaver of Worlds* series is especially close to my heart because it continues the magical journey that began with your name and spirit woven into every stitch of the tale.

You inspired this world—a place filled with courage, creativity, and compassion. Just like the Heart Weaver herself, you have a unique light that brings things to life, lifts those around you, and makes the world better simply by being in it. I hope you enjoy this next chapter as much as I enjoyed crafting it for you.

May these pages remind you of how truly special you are, and may they carry you to a place where imagination has no limits.

With all my love,
Dad-Dad

Table of contents

Contents

Chapter 1: Threads of New Beginnings

The air in Solara was a symphony. Not just the melodious singing that had returned to the sapphire forests, a constant, joyful hum that resonated deep within Mia's bones, but a chorus of scents, textures, and lights. It was the sweet, heady perfume of the glowing flora, a fragrance unlike any flower on Earth, mingled with the crisp, clean tang of the mountain air and the subtle, metallic scent of ancient, vibrant magic. It was the soft, springy give of the moss beneath her feet, the cool, smooth touch of sapphire leaves as she brushed past them, and the warm, gentle pulse of the twin moons, now shining with a brilliance that painted the landscape in hues of silver and violet. This was home.

It had been weeks since the defeat of Malakor, since the grand weaving at the Whispering Falls had purified the land and sent the dark sorcerer into oblivion. Weeks since Dreadwing, freed from his malevolent enchantment, had soared into the Solaraean sky, a majestic, sorrowful silhouette against the twin moons, before vanishing into the distant peaks, seeking solace and healing. Weeks since Queen Sasha had been restored to her throne, her frail form replaced by a regal bearing, her eyes shining with the renewed hope of her people.

And weeks since Mia Martinez, the graphic designer from Boerne, Texas, and Ethan Morgan, her steadfast engineer, had chosen to remain.

Their decision had been met with an outpouring of joy and gratitude from the Solaraean people. Mia, the Heart Weaver, was revered, her rosewood needles now a symbol of hope and restoration. Ethan, her loyal companion, was admired for his unwavering support and his curious, practical mind. They were no longer outsiders; they were integral threads in the grand tapestry of Solara.

Yet, the transition wasn't without its complexities. The sheer, overwhelming beauty of Solara, its constant magical hum, was a stark contrast to the familiar, mundane rhythm of Newark, Arkansas. Mia often found herself pausing, simply to breathe in the luminous air, to watch the sapphire trees shimmer, to listen to the ceaseless, ethereal music of the land. It was a world that demanded constant engagement, a sensory feast that sometimes left her delightfully overwhelmed.

Their new residence was within the shimmering castle, no longer a place of oppressive gloom but a beacon of light and life. Queen Sasha had insisted they take a suite of rooms overlooking the restored Royal Gardens, a vibrant expanse of glowing flora and sapphire trees that pulsed with renewed vitality. The castle itself, once a dark, foreboding fortress, now felt alive, its ancient stones humming with benevolent magic. Sunlight, filtered through crystalline windows, danced across polished floors, and the air was filled with the soft murmur of Solaraean voices, the gentle clinking of chimes, and the occasional melodic laughter of children.

Mia's days were now dedicated to the subtle art of mending. Her role as Heart Weaver was less about grand, dramatic confrontations and more about delicate, intricate restoration. Queen Sasha, wise and patient, guided her, explaining the nuances of Solaraean magic, the delicate balance of its ecosystems, and the profound connection between the land and its inhabitants.

One morning, Mia found herself in a secluded glade within the Royal Gardens, her rosewood needles humming with a soft, comforting warmth in her hands. Before her lay a patch of glowing flora, its petals muted, their usual vibrant pulse diminished to a faint, erratic flicker. A small cluster of Solaraean children, their eyes wide with curiosity, watched her from a respectful distance, their tiny knitted companions – miniature versions of Hopsy, a testament to Mia's earlier, accidental creations – perched on their shoulders.

"This section was particularly affected by Malakor's influence," Queen Sasha explained, her voice soft, her hand gently brushing a wilting petal. "His darkness sought to drain the very life from our light-bearing flora. It is not malicious now, merely… exhausted. It needs its vibrancy rewoven."

Mia nodded, understanding. She chose a skein of yarn the color of fresh emeralds, its fibers shimmering with an inner light. She focused, not on a grand illusion, but on the essence of life, of growth, of restorative energy. Her fingers moved with practiced ease, each stitch a deliberate act of mending. She wove a delicate, almost invisible thread around the base of each wilting plant, connecting them, creating a subtle, intricate network of healing energy.

As she worked, the emerald yarn seemed to melt into the flora, becoming one with its essence. The muted petals began to unfurl, their colors deepening, their internal lights pulsing with renewed vigor. A faint, sweet perfume, stronger than before, wafted through the glade. The children gasped, their faces alight with wonder, their knitted companions twitching their noses in delight.

It was slow, painstaking work, requiring immense concentration and a deep connection to the land. Mia felt the energy flow from her, through the needles, into the plants, a gentle, reciprocal exchange. When she finally tied off the last knot, the patch of flora glowed with a brilliance that rivaled the morning sun, its petals unfurling in a silent, joyful dance.

"It is beautiful, Weaver," Queen Sasha said, her voice filled with quiet awe. "You have brought life back to them."

Mia smiled, a genuine, radiant smile that reached her eyes. This was her purpose. This was the Heart Weaver's true calling. It wasn't about fighting dragons, but about nurturing life, about ensuring Solara's harmony endured. The subtle hum of her needles, once a bewildering anomaly, was now a constant, comforting presence, a reminder of the profound connection she shared with this magical world.

While Mia immersed herself in the subtle art of magical restoration, Ethan, ever the pragmatist, found his own unique role. His engineering mind, accustomed to the rigid laws of physics and the predictable mechanics of the mundane world, was now playfully grappling with the boundless, illogical possibilities of magic. He saw Solara not just as a place of wonder, but as a vast, complex system, a grand machine waiting to be understood and optimized.

His workshop, a cavernous space within the castle's lower levels that had once been a forgotten storage area, was now a fascinating blend of earthly ingenuity and Solaraean enchantment. Blueprints for fantastical devices were tacked to the walls alongside sketches of complex gear systems. Strange, glowing Solaraean crystals lay on his workbench next to his familiar wrench set and a multimeter.

One of his first projects involved the castle's internal water system. Before Malakor, the castle had been supplied by a series of magically enchanted aqueducts that drew water from a hidden underground spring, purifying and enriching it as it flowed. Malakor's influence had disrupted these enchantments, leaving parts of the castle with stagnant, muted water.

"It's like a magical plumbing system," Ethan explained to Mia one afternoon, his face smudged with iridescent dust, his eyes alight with the thrill of a new challenge. "The water still flows, but the enchantments are… clogged, for lack of a better term. The magical resonance is off. If we can re-route some of the energy, or perhaps introduce a new conduit, we can get the old system humming again."

Mia watched him, fascinated, as he meticulously examined a section of the aqueduct, a glowing Solaraean crystal held to his ear, listening for faint magical frequencies. He was applying logic to magic, bridging the gap between two seemingly disparate worlds.

"Can your needles help?" Ethan asked, looking up at her. "Maybe knit a new conduit? Something that can channel pure magical energy?"

Mia considered. Her magic could create, could transform, could mend. Could it also conduct? It was a new application, but the idea intrigued her. She pulled out a skein of shimmering, almost translucent silver yarn, the kind she used for her most ethereal creations. She focused on conduction, flow, purity . She began to knit a long, delicate, almost invisible thread, imbued with the property of magical conductivity.

As she knitted, the silver thread shimmered, pulsing with a faint, internal light, like a tiny, liquid stream of starlight. It felt cool and smooth, yet vibrated with a subtle energy. Ethan, watching her, carefully attached one end of the knitted conduit to a section of the aqueduct, then, following his calculations, connected the other end to a naturally occurring magical ley line he had discovered beneath the castle.

The moment the connection was made, a surge of vibrant, emerald light pulsed through Mia's knitted conduit. The aqueduct hummed, its ancient enchantments flickering, then strengthening. The water within, once murky and still, began to swirl with renewed vigor, its surface shimmering with iridescent light. A fresh, clean scent, like a mountain spring, filled the workshop.

"It worked!" Ethan exclaimed, a triumphant grin spreading across his face. "You knitted a magical wire, Mia! This is incredible!"

Mia felt a surge of pride and exhilaration. Her magic was adapting, growing, finding new applications beyond her wildest imagination. Together, they were building a new Solara, one where ancient magic and modern ingenuity could coexist, even enhance each other.

Life in the castle quickly settled into a comfortable rhythm. The Solaraean people were warm, welcoming, and endlessly curious about their new Heart Weaver and her companion. They were a people deeply connected to their land, their lives intertwined with its magical pulse. Their customs were simple, yet profound: daily communal meals filled with melodic conversation, evening gatherings where ancient tales were spun in song, and quiet moments of reverence for the twin moons and the glowing flora.

Mia found herself drawn into their gentle way of life. She learned their language, a melodic tongue filled with soft vowels and resonant consonants, surprisingly easy to pick up with the subtle magical assistance of the land itself. She shared stories of Earth, of Newark, of the mundane world they had left behind, always careful to highlight the beauty and wonder of their own reality, rather than dwelling on the stark contrasts.

Bean, after her initial disorientation, had adapted with surprising ease. She loved the endless, glowing moss of the Royal Gardens, chasing after the tiny, ethereal sprites that flitted through the sapphire trees. She had even made friends with a few of the smaller, shy, furry creatures that resembled oversized squirrels, engaging in playful chases through the castle grounds. Hopsy, the knitted rabbit, remained her constant companion, often perched on her head or nestled in her fur, its button eyes wide with endless curiosity.

The Solaraean children, in particular, adored Mia. They would gather around her, their eyes wide with wonder, as she knitted small, animated toys for them – tiny, fluttering birds, scurrying mice, and miniature versions of Hopsy, each one imbued with a spark of life and a unique personality. These creations, unlike the larger, more purposeful ones, were pure joy, simple acts of creation that brought laughter and delight to the castle. Mia found a deep satisfaction in these moments, a quiet happiness that transcended the grander responsibilities of her role.

Despite the restoration, a subtle undercurrent of sorrow lingered in Solara, a quiet echo of the darkness it had endured. The grief for Bear, Mia's loyal golden retriever, was a constant, dull ache in her heart. She often found herself looking for his lumbering presence, his golden fur, his comforting sigh. She knew he had sacrificed himself for them, a brave and selfless act, and she carried his memory like a precious, painful jewel. Ethan, too, felt his absence keenly, often pausing in his work, his gaze drifting to the empty space where Bear would usually be sprawled.

One evening, as the twin moons cast long, shimmering shadows across the Royal Gardens, Mia sat with Queen Sasha on a bench carved from luminous stone. The air was cool, filled with the soft music of the land and the gentle hum of the restored flora.

"He was a brave companion," Queen Sasha said softly, sensing Mia's quiet melancholy. "His spirit… it is woven into the very fabric of Solara now. His courage will forever resonate within our land."

Mia nodded, tears pricking her eyes. "I miss him. So much."

"Grief is a thread, Weaver," the Queen replied, her voice filled with ancient wisdom. "It is a dark thread, yes, but it is also a thread of love. And love, too, can be woven into the tapestry. It can strengthen it, make it more beautiful, more resilient."

Mia found solace in the Queen's words, in the Solaraean understanding of life and loss. She began to knit a small, intricate pattern, a memorial to Bear, weaving his golden fur (from a skein of yarn she had magically imbued with his color) into a shimmering, ethereal tapestry that would hang in their chambers, a constant reminder of his love and sacrifice. It was a private act of mending, not for the land, but for her own heart.

As the weeks turned into months, Solara continued to heal. The sapphire trees grew taller, their leaves shimmering with renewed brilliance. The glowing flora bloomed with vibrant intensity. The melodious singing returned to the forests, a constant symphony of joy. The twin moons shone brighter, their combined light illuminating a land reborn.

Yet, amidst this burgeoning harmony, subtle disturbances began to manifest. They were not malicious, not the oppressive darkness of Malakor, but unsettling nonetheless. They were like faint, discordant notes in Solara's otherwise perfect symphony.

Mia, attuned to the magical pulse of the land through her needles, was the first to notice. One afternoon, while mending a patch of shimmering moss near a crystal stream, she felt a faint, unfamiliar resonance through her needles. It was a subtle vibration, different from the comforting hum of Solara's natural magic, and distinct from the malevolent thrum of Malakor's dark influence. This was… a flicker. A brief, almost imperceptible *unraveling* of a single thread in the grand tapestry.

She dismissed it at first, attributing it to lingering magical residue from Malakor, or perhaps her own fatigue. But the feeling returned. A few days later, while she was helping Queen Sasha restore the vibrancy of a muted waterfall, the water, for a fleeting moment, lost its iridescent shimmer, becoming dull and opaque before snapping back to its usual brilliance. It was so quick, so subtle, that only Mia, with her heightened senses, seemed to notice.

"Did you see that?" Mia asked Queen Sasha, her brow furrowed.

Queen Sasha paused, her gaze fixed on the waterfall. "See what, my dear?"

"The water," Mia explained, pointing. "It just… went dull for a second. Like the light flickered out."

Queen Sasha studied the waterfall, then shook her head gently. "I confess, Weaver, I saw nothing amiss. The falls are vibrant." Her ancient eyes, however, held a hint of concern, a subtle shift in her expression. She trusted Mia's senses implicitly.

Ethan, too, began to notice small, inexplicable anomalies. He was working on a new project: designing a system of magically reinforced pathways that would allow Solaraean children to safely explore the higher branches of the sapphire trees. He was using a blend of Mia's magically conductive yarn and naturally occurring Solaraean crystals to create stable, levitating platforms.

One morning, while calibrating a newly installed platform, his instruments, usually precise, gave him a momentary, unexplainable reading. The magical energy flowing through the platform briefly dipped, then surged, before returning to normal. It was a tiny blip, easily dismissed as a glitch, but Ethan's engineer's intuition told him otherwise.

"That's odd," he muttered, re-checking his readings. "The energy flow just… hiccupped. Like a momentary power surge, but in reverse."

He tried to replicate it, but the platform hummed steadily, its magic flowing smoothly. He made a note in his journal, a question mark beside the anomaly.

The Solaraean people, too, began to express minor, unexplainable concerns. A farmer reported that a patch of his luminescent crops, usually robust, had briefly lost their glow, only to recover within minutes. A musician complained that her instrument, usually perfectly attuned to Solara's melodic hum, had briefly played a jarring, off-key note before correcting itself. These were not crises, not widespread problems, but isolated incidents, small whispers of discord in an otherwise harmonious land.

"It is nothing, Weaver," a Solaraean elder, a woman with eyes like polished emeralds, assured Mia one day, after Mia inquired about a brief, localized silence in the forest melodies she had perceived. "The land is healing. Perhaps the echoes of Malakor's darkness still linger, like a bad dream. They will fade."

But Mia wasn't so sure. The resonance she felt through her needles was different. It wasn't the cold, sharp presence of Malakor's malevolence. It was more akin to a faint, almost imperceptible *tremor*. Like a foundational stone shifting, or a single thread in a vast tapestry subtly fraying, not due to an external attack, but from an internal, structural stress.

She spent more time in quiet contemplation, her needles resting in her lap, her senses open to Solara's magical pulse. She felt the vibrant flow of energy, the deep, resonant hum of the land, the joyous symphony of its life. But beneath it all, like a barely audible undertone, she detected a faint, rhythmic *skip*. A tiny, almost imperceptible pause in the flow. A momentary *unraveling*.

It was too subtle to be a threat, too fleeting to be a crisis. But it was there. A puzzle. A whisper of something deeper, something that suggested Malakor's defeat was not the end of Solara's challenges, but merely the end of one chapter. The land was restored, yes, but perhaps its very foundations, its ancient magical core, had suffered a deeper, more insidious wound, one that was only now beginning to manifest.

One evening, as the twin moons cast their ethereal glow across the Royal Gardens, Mia sat with Ethan, watching Hopsy chase after a glowing beetle. The air was filled with the soft, melodic hum of the land, a comforting lullaby.

"I keep feeling it," Mia confessed, her voice low. "A flicker. A tiny skip in the magic. It's not like Malakor. It's… different. Like something is subtly off-kilter."

Ethan, ever the analytical one, nodded slowly. "I've noticed it too. Small anomalies. My instruments pick up brief energy fluctuations that don't make sense. It's not a power surge, it's more like… a momentary instability. A resonance that's just slightly out of tune."

He looked at Mia, his eyes thoughtful. "You said Solara's magic flows like rivers. What if… what if some of those rivers are getting blocked? Or their currents are subtly changing?"

Mia picked up her rosewood needles, their warmth a familiar comfort. The faint, rhythmic skip was there again, a subtle tremor beneath her fingertips. It was a quiet, persistent hum, a question whispered by the land itself.

"I don't know," Mia admitted, her gaze drifting towards the distant, shimmering peaks, where Dreadwing had vanished. "But I have a feeling… this is just the beginning."

The tapestry of their lives in Solara had been rewoven, vibrant and beautiful. But Mia, the Heart Weaver, knew that a truly grand tapestry was never truly finished. There were always new threads to weave, new patterns to discover, and new harmonies to restore. And sometimes, even in the most beautiful of tapestries, a single, subtle thread could begin to unravel, hinting at a deeper, more complex story yet to unfold. The echoes of Solara were beginning to whisper, and Mia, with her sensitive needles and her unwavering heart, was ready to listen.

Chapter 2: Whispers on the Wind

The initial weeks of harmonious restoration had slowly given way to a quiet disquiet. The vibrant symphony of Solara, once a flawless composition, now held faint, almost imperceptible discords. These were not the jarring, malevolent notes of Malakor's influence, but subtle, unsettling tremors, like a beloved instrument playing a fraction of a tone flat, or a single thread in a grand tapestry subtly fraying, not due to an external attack, but from an internal, structural stress. Mia, the Heart Weaver, with her heightened sensitivity to the land's magical pulse, felt these anomalies first, a faint, unfamiliar resonance through her rosewood needles.

One crisp Solaraean morning, as the twin moons still lingered faintly in the indigo sky, Mia walked through a section of the Royal Gardens she had personally mended weeks prior. The glowing flora here had been particularly vibrant, its petals unfurling in a silent, joyful dance, its inner light pulsing with renewed vigor. Today, however, as she approached, a subtle shift caught her eye. A cluster of what the Solaraeans called 'Sun-Kissed Lilies,' usually a riot of incandescent gold, seemed momentarily muted. Their vibrant glow flickered, dimmed to a dull, sickly yellow, and then, just as quickly, surged back to their usual brilliance. It was so fleeting, so subtle, that anyone less attuned to the land's magic would have dismissed it as a trick of the light. But Mia felt it, a faint, almost imperceptible *void* through her needles, a momentary absence where magic should have been.

Her needles, usually humming with a comforting warmth, felt a fleeting chill, a sensation akin to a sudden drop in air pressure. She knelt, her fingers brushing the petals of a lily. The magic felt strong, vibrant, yet the memory of that brief, unsettling flicker lingered. She tried to mend it, focusing on the essence of life and growth, but the lily, already vibrant, offered no resistance, accepted no new energy. It was as if the problem wasn't a wound to be healed, but a fleeting instability, a momentary loss of connection.

Later that day, while observing Ethan in his workshop, a similar anomaly occurred. He was meticulously calibrating a new series of magically reinforced pathways designed to allow Solaraean children to safely explore the higher branches of the sapphire trees. These pathways, woven from Mia's magically conductive yarn and naturally occurring Solaraean crystals, hummed with a steady, emerald light, providing stable, levitating platforms. Ethan, ever the engineer, was using a complex array of Solaraean crystals and modified Earth instruments to measure the magical energy flow.

Suddenly, a small, crystalline device on his workbench, designed to measure magical resonance, emitted a sharp, discordant *ping*. The emerald light in the pathway flickered, dipped to a dull, almost grey hue, and then surged back, brighter than before. Ethan's brow furrowed. "That's odd," he muttered, re-checking his readings. "The energy flow just… hiccupped. Like a momentary power surge, but in reverse. A sudden drain, then an overcompensation." He tapped the device, then the pathway. Both hummed steadily, their magic flowing smoothly. He made a note in his journal, a question mark beside the anomaly, a tiny imperfection in his otherwise perfectly logical system.

"Did you feel that, Mia?" he asked, looking up. "A brief dip in the magical current?"

Mia nodded, her own needles having registered the subtle tremor. "Yes. It was like… a thread snapping, then instantly re-forming. Not broken, just… disconnected for a second."

They exchanged a look, a shared understanding passing between them. These incidents were no longer isolated. They were becoming more frequent, more pronounced, subtle whispers that hinted at a deeper, more pervasive issue.

The Solaraean people, while resilient and accustomed to the ebb and flow of magic, began to express minor, unexplainable concerns. A farmer from the outskirts of the Royal City, a man named Kael, with hands as gnarled as ancient roots, approached Mia during her morning rounds. "Weaver," he began, his voice hesitant, "my luminescent crops… the Sun-Glow Wheat. Usually, it pulses with a steady, golden light, even at night. But lately, sometimes, for a breath, the glow dims. Like a candle flickering in a draft. Then it returns. It is not harmful, but… unsettling."

Mia listened, her heart sinking. She had seen the Sun-Glow Wheat, its fields a breathtaking sea of shimmering gold. For it to dim, even for a moment, was significant.

Later, during an evening gathering in the castle's grand hall, where Solaraean musicians filled the air with their melodic singing, a jarring note pierced the harmony. Elara, a renowned Solaraean harpist, her fingers usually dancing effortlessly across the glowing strings of her instrument, gasped. Her harp, usually perfectly attuned to Solara's melodic hum, had briefly played a jarring, off-key note, a dissonant chord that grated against the ears before correcting itself. Elara frowned, her brow furrowed in confusion, then shrugged it off as a momentary lapse in concentration. But Mia, sitting nearby, felt the tremor through her very soul, a brief, painful jolt that resonated with the unsettling flicker she had felt in the gardens.

These were not crises, not widespread problems, but isolated incidents, small whispers of discord in an otherwise harmonious land. The elders, wise and ancient, would often dismiss them. "It is nothing, Weaver," an elder named Lyra, a woman with eyes like polished emeralds and hair like spun moonlight, assured Mia one day. "The land is healing. Perhaps the echoes of Malakor's darkness still linger, like a bad dream. They will fade. Solara has known greater trials."

But Mia wasn't so sure. The resonance she felt through her needles was different. It wasn't the cold, sharp presence of Malakor's malevolence. That had been a tangible, oppressive weight, a darkness that sought to consume. This was more akin to a faint, almost imperceptible *tremor*. Like a foundational stone shifting, or a single thread in a vast tapestry subtly fraying, not due to an external attack, but from an internal, structural stress. It was a feeling of *emptiness*, a momentary void where the vibrant magical current should have been.

She spent more time in quiet contemplation, her needles resting in her lap, her senses open to Solara's magical pulse. She felt the vibrant flow of energy, the deep, resonant hum of the land, the joyous symphony of its life. But beneath it all, like a barely audible undertone, she detected a faint, rhythmic *skip*. A tiny, almost imperceptible pause in the flow. A momentary *unraveling*. It was too subtle to be a threat, too fleeting to be a crisis. But it was there. A puzzle. A whisper of something deeper, something that suggested Malakor's defeat was not the end of Solara's challenges, but merely the end of one chapter. The land was restored, yes, but perhaps its very foundations, its ancient magical core, had suffered a deeper, more insidious wound, one that was only now beginning to manifest.

Mia confided in Ethan, her voice hushed with concern. "It's like the land is holding its breath for a second, then exhaling too quickly. The magic isn't flowing smoothly anymore. It's… stuttering."

Ethan, ever the analytical one, nodded slowly. He had been meticulously logging his instrument readings, charting the anomalies. "The data supports it, Mia. These aren't random glitches. There's a pattern, albeit a subtle one. The energy fluctuations are too consistent to be residual noise from Malakor. It's a systemic issue. Like a circuit breaker tripping, but only for a millisecond, and then resetting itself."

They decided to investigate further, to see if they could pinpoint the source of these subtle disturbances. Their first thought was to revisit areas that had been most heavily affected by Malakor's reign, theorizing that perhaps the healing was incomplete, or that some deep-seated corruption remained.

They ventured into the outskirts of the sapphire forest, a place that had been particularly blighted by the sorcerer's darkness. Here, the trees had been twisted and gnarled, their sapphire leaves muted to a dull, sickly blue. Mia had spent weeks painstakingly reweaving the life back into them, her emerald yarn flowing into their very essence, restoring their vibrancy. Now, they shimmered with renewed brilliance, their leaves a vibrant, pulsing sapphire.

As they walked, Bean darted ahead, chasing after a group of tiny, glowing sprites that flitted through the undergrowth. Hopsy, perched on Mia's shoulder, twitched its nose, its button eyes wide and alert. The forest hummed with its usual melodic song, a comforting presence.

Suddenly, Bean whimpered. She stopped dead in her tracks, her ears flattening, her tail drooping. The sprites she had been chasing flickered, their tiny lights dimming, and then, with a soft *pop*, vanished entirely. The melodic hum of the forest in that immediate vicinity faltered, replaced by a momentary, unsettling silence, a void in the symphony of Solara.

Mia felt it through her needles, a sharp, cold *absence*, far more pronounced than the subtle flickers she had felt before. It was like a sudden, unexpected drop into an empty space. Her needles vibrated with a frantic, unfamiliar resonance, a sensation that was neither warm nor cold, but utterly hollow.

Ethan, seeing Bean's reaction and Mia's sudden pallor, rushed forward. "What is it?"

"The magic," Mia whispered, her voice strained. "It just… disappeared. For a second. The sprites… they're gone." She looked around, her eyes searching for any sign of the tiny creatures. Nothing. The silence in that small patch of forest was unnerving, a stark contrast to the vibrant life around it.

Mia knelt, her hands hovering over the moss where the sprites had vanished. Her needles pulsed, trying to grasp at something, to find a thread to mend, but there was nothing. No wound, no tear, just… absence.

"It's like a localized magical vacuum," Ethan mused, pulling out his instruments. His resonance meter, usually so precise, was wildly fluctuating, unable to get a stable reading in that spot. "The energy isn't just dipping; it's being momentarily *nullified*."

They spent the rest of the day in that section of the forest, observing. The silence would return intermittently, lasting for a few seconds, then receding, allowing the forest's melody to resume. Each time, Mia felt that hollow, unsettling resonance through her needles, a feeling of deep unease. It wasn't Malakor's darkness. It was something else. Something systemic.

"It's not a malevolent force," Mia concluded later that evening, back in the safety of their castle suite, her needles still faintly trembling. "It doesn't feel like an attack. It feels… like a glitch. Like the land is having a seizure, a momentary loss of control over its own magic."

Ethan nodded, reviewing his data. "The energy readings are consistent with a localized, transient magical instability. Not an external drain, but an internal malfunction. Like a heart skipping a beat."

Their conversations with Queen Sasha and the Solaraean elders proved frustrating. While they listened patiently, their ancient wisdom seemed to frame these incidents within the context of Solara's long history of magical ebb and flow.

"The land breathes, Weaver," Lyra, the elder with emerald eyes, explained gently. "Sometimes, its breath is shallow. Sometimes, it is deep. After such a great darkness, it is natural for the land to find its new rhythm. These are but the echoes of its recovery."

"But it feels different," Mia insisted, trying to convey the subtle, unsettling sensation. "It's not an echo of Malakor. It's… an unraveling. Like the very threads of magic are momentarily losing their cohesion."

Queen Sasha, though she trusted Mia's intuition implicitly, seemed hesitant to accept such a dire interpretation. "Solara has always been resilient, Weaver. Its magic, though tested, has always found its balance. Perhaps your heightened senses, new to our world, perceive these natural fluctuations with a greater intensity."

Mia understood their perspective. They had lived through countless cycles of magical flux. They had just endured Malakor's reign, a profound trauma from which the land was still recovering. To suggest a new, systemic problem, one that was internal to Solara itself, was a difficult truth to accept. It implied a vulnerability they hadn't known existed.

But Mia couldn't shake the feeling. The anomalies were becoming slightly more frequent, affecting slightly larger areas. A small section of a sapphire forest, where the leaves briefly lost their shimmer, turning dull and lifeless before snapping back to their vibrant hue. A small, natural spring whose water briefly lost its purifying properties, becoming murky and stagnant before clearing again.

The Solaraean people, while still largely attributing these incidents to minor issues or lingering magical residue, began to show a subtle unease. The melodic singing in the forests, while still constant, would occasionally be punctuated by these brief, unsettling silences. The glowing flora, while still beautiful, would sometimes flicker with an almost desperate energy.

Mia's internal struggle intensified. Was she overreacting? Was her unique connection to the land, her role as Heart Weaver, making her perceive problems where none truly existed? Or was she seeing a truth that others, accustomed to Solara's magical fluctuations, were simply overlooking?

She spent hours by herself, her needles resting in her lap, her senses open to Solara's magical pulse. She felt the vibrant flow of energy, the deep, resonant hum of the land, the joyous symphony of its life. But beneath it all, like a barely audible undertone, she detected that faint, rhythmic *skip*. A tiny, almost imperceptible pause in the flow. A momentary *unraveling*.

The feeling through her needles was becoming more distinct. It wasn't cold, not hot, but a profound sense of *emptiness*, a void where magic should be. It was like a momentary tear in the fabric of reality itself, instantly mended, but leaving a faint scar, a lingering tremor.

She tried to mend one of these "skips" directly. She found a small, glowing rock formation that had briefly dimmed, its internal light flickering. She focused her magic, channeling restorative energy through her needles, intending to reinforce its magical structure. But as her magic flowed, instead of strengthening the rock, it seemed to *exacerbate* the flicker. The rock's light dimmed further, then pulsed erratically, before finally stabilizing, leaving Mia feeling disproportionately drained. Her current mending techniques, designed for damage and corruption, were ineffective against this new kind of instability. It was like trying to patch a hole in a river with a needle and thread; the current simply flowed around it, or worse, pulled the thread away.

This confirmed her growing suspicion: the problem was not damage to be mended, but a fundamental imbalance, a subtle shift in the very resonance of Solara's magical core. Her weaving was about harmony, about bringing things into balance. But to balance something, you first had to understand why it was out of alignment.

One evening, as the twin moons cast their ethereal glow across the Royal Gardens, Mia sat with Ethan, watching Hopsy chase after a glowing beetle, its tiny knitted legs a blur. The air was filled with the soft, melodic hum of the land, a comforting lullaby, yet Mia could still feel the faint, rhythmic skip beneath it all.

"I keep feeling it," Mia confessed, her voice low, her frustration evident. "A flicker. A tiny skip in the magic. It's not like Malakor. It's… different. Like something is subtly off-kilter. And my mending isn't working on it. It's like I'm trying to fix a broken clock by polishing its hands. The problem is deeper."

Ethan, ever the analytical one, nodded slowly. He had been meticulously logging his instrument readings, charting the anomalies. "The data supports it, Mia. These aren't random glitches. There's a pattern, albeit a subtle one. The energy fluctuations are too consistent to be residual noise from Malakor. It's a systemic issue. Like a circuit breaker tripping, but only for a millisecond, and then resetting itself. And your experience with the glowing rock confirms it's not a simple repair job."

He looked at Mia, his eyes thoughtful. "You said Solara's magic flows like rivers. What if… what if some of those rivers are getting blocked? Or their currents are subtly changing? What if the entire magical aquifer is slowly losing pressure, or its channels are shifting?"

Mia picked up her rosewood needles, their warmth a familiar comfort, but also a silent question. The faint, rhythmic skip was there again, a subtle tremor beneath her fingertips. It was a quiet, persistent hum, a question whispered by the land itself.

"It's like Solara itself is slowly, imperceptibly, coming undone from within," Mia admitted, the realization settling heavily in her chest. "Not being attacked, but… unraveling. And my magic, while it can mend, it can't re-engineer. I can fix a broken thread, but I can't re-design the entire loom."

Ethan's eyes widened. "Re-design the loom. That's it. This isn't a battle against a villain, Mia. This is… a fundamental re-calibration. A deep-seated imbalance that Malakor might have exacerbated, but didn't create. It's an internal problem, not an external one."

The gravity of their realization settled between them. Malakor had been a clear, tangible enemy. This new threat was insidious, a slow, internal decay that affected the very essence of Solara. It wasn't a dragon to fight, or a sorcerer to defeat. It was the land itself, subtly losing its harmony.

"So, what do we do?" Mia asked, her voice quiet, but filled with a new resolve. The fear was still there, but it was overshadowed by a profound sense of purpose. This was her calling, her destiny as the Heart Weaver.

Ethan leaned forward, his engineer's mind already whirring, grappling with the immense complexity of the problem. "We need more information. We need to understand Solara's magical foundations, its ancient core. How it was originally woven, how it maintains its balance. We need blueprints for the loom itself, not just instructions for mending its threads."

He paused, then looked at her, a flicker of excitement in his eyes. "Queen Sasha mentioned ancient prophecies, forgotten places. There has to be a source of knowledge, a place where the original weavers stored their wisdom. Something that can tell us how to re-tune Solara's core."

Mia's gaze drifted towards the distant, shimmering peaks, where Dreadwing had vanished, and beyond, to the uncharted territories of Solara. The tapestry of their lives in Solara had been rewoven, vibrant and beautiful. But Mia, the Heart Weaver, knew that a truly grand tapestry was never truly finished. There were always new threads to weave, new patterns to discover, and new harmonies to restore. And sometimes, even in the most beautiful of tapestries, a single, subtle thread could begin to unravel, hinting at a deeper, more complex story yet to unfold. The echoes of Solara were beginning to whisper, not of a new enemy, but of a profound, ancient imbalance. And Mia, with her sensitive needles and her unwavering heart, was ready to listen, ready to seek the knowledge that would allow her to reweave Solara's very essence, to ensure its enduring harmony. This was just the beginning of their true adventure, a quest not of combat, but of profound understanding and ultimate restoration.

Chapter 3: The Unraveling Bloom

The whispers had grown louder, the subtle discords more pronounced. What began as fleeting flickers in the Sun-Kissed Lilies and momentary dips in the sapphire tree pathways had escalated into a more tangible, unsettling phenomenon. The land, which had so recently hummed with restored vitality, now seemed to hold its breath in certain places, exhaling a quiet sigh of distress. Mia's needles, once a comforting presence, now trembled with a constant, low thrum, a sympathetic vibration to Solara's growing unease.

The first truly alarming sign manifested in the **Luminous Bloom Fields**, a vast expanse of glowing flora that stretched for miles beyond the Royal City. These fields were Solara's primary source of light-bearing sustenance, their radiant petals harvested for food, medicine, and the very energy that powered many Solaraean homes. They were a breathtaking spectacle, a sea of pulsating, vibrant colors that shifted with the twin moons' cycles, a testament to Solara's inherent magic.

One morning, a frantic messenger arrived at the castle, his face etched with worry. "Weaver! Engineer! Your Majesties!" he gasped, bowing deeply, his voice trembling. "The Luminous Bloom Fields… they are sickening! The glow… it is fading!"

Mia and Ethan rushed to the fields, Queen Sasha accompanying them, her regal composure strained by a visible tremor of concern. The sight that greeted them was heartbreaking. Where once had been a kaleidoscope of incandescent light, now lay vast swathes of muted, dull flora. The vibrant reds had faded to a sickly rust, the brilliant blues to a murky grey, and the golden pulses were reduced to a faint, erratic flicker, like dying embers. The melodic hum that usually emanated from the fields, a gentle, soothing song, was replaced by a low, mournful sigh, a sound of deep, pervasive distress.

Farmers stood among their wilting crops, their faces despairing, their hands hovering helplessly over the dying blooms. The air, usually sweet with the perfume of the flora, now carried a faint, acrid scent, like something slowly decaying.

Mia knelt amidst the dying blooms, her heart aching. Her needles vibrated fiercely, a frantic, desperate pulse against her palm. She reached out, her fingers brushing a wilting petal of a once-vibrant Crimson Bloom. The magic felt weak, almost nonexistent, a faint, struggling current against an overwhelming tide of… nothingness. It wasn't corruption, not

Malakor's malevolence. It was an **absence**. A profound, terrifying void where magic should have been.

"It's not a blight," Mia whispered, her voice tight with concern. "It's like the magic is simply… draining away. As if the very essence of their light is being siphoned off."

Ethan, ever the scientist, pulled out his instruments. His resonance meter, which had previously shown only fleeting anomalies, now registered a consistent, alarming drop in magical energy across the entire field. "The magical resonance here is plummeting," he stated, his voice grim. "It's like a massive leak in the system. The energy isn't just fluctuating; it's actively disappearing." He ran a small, crystalline scanner over a wilting bloom. The scanner, designed to analyze magical composition, showed a rapid degradation of the flora's inherent magical structure. The intricate, interwoven threads of light that formed its very being were simply… unraveling.

Queen Sasha walked among her people, offering words of comfort, but her eyes, usually filled with serene wisdom, now held a deep, profound sadness. "The Luminous Blooms… they are the heart of our land's sustenance. Without their light, our people will weaken. Our very spirit will dim." Her voice was heavy with the weight of her kingdom's plight.

Mia knew she had to act. This was no longer a subtle whisper; it was a desperate cry. She chose a skein of yarn, a vibrant, life-affirming green, and began to knit. She focused on **restoration, replenishment, binding**. She poured her magic into the stitches, weaving a delicate, intricate network of healing threads, intending to infuse the dying blooms with renewed vitality, to bind their unraveling essence.

She worked for hours, moving from bloom to bloom, her fingers a blur of motion, her needles humming with furious energy. She wove threads of vibrant green into the muted petals, around the wilting stems, connecting them, creating a subtle, intricate web of restorative magic. She felt the drain on her own energy, a profound weariness creeping into her bones, but she pushed through, driven by a desperate need to save the blooms.

But as she worked, a chilling realization dawned. Her mending, while it momentarily brightened the blooms, did not hold. The vibrant green threads she wove would pulse with light for a few minutes, the petals would regain a fleeting hint of their former glory, but then, slowly, inexorably, the dullness would return. The green threads would dim, their magic dissipating, and the unraveling would continue. It was like pouring water into a sieve; the magic simply flowed through, unable to bind, unable to hold.

Mia felt a surge of despair. Her power, which had defeated Malakor, which had restored the castle's aqueducts and brought life back to the glade, was failing. It was like trying to mend a torn piece of fabric when the very fibers of the fabric itself were dissolving.

"It's not working," Mia whispered, her voice hoarse, her hands trembling with exhaustion and frustration. "My mending… it won't hold. The magic just… seeps away. It's like the blooms can't *contain* the magic anymore. They're losing their ability to hold the threads together."

Ethan knelt beside her, his face grim. He examined a bloom Mia had just worked on. The energy readings, after a brief spike, were indeed plummeting again. "You're right. It's not a wound you can patch. It's a fundamental structural failure. Like the magical equivalent of cellular decay. The very weave of their being is coming apart."

Queen Sasha, observing Mia's struggle, approached them, her expression filled with a deep, ancient sorrow. "This is worse than Malakor's blight," she murmured, her gaze sweeping across the dying fields. "His darkness sought to corrupt. This… this is a slow death from within. A return to the Great Silence."

The Great Silence. The term sent a shiver down Mia's spine. It spoke of a time before Solara's vibrant magic, a time of emptiness and void.

A council was called in the castle's grand hall. The Solaraean elders, their faces somber, gathered with Queen Sasha, Mia, and Ethan. The air was heavy with unspoken fear, a palpable sense of dread that permeated the usually vibrant hall.

Lyra, the elder with emerald eyes, spoke first, her voice low and resonant. "The Luminous Blooms are not merely plants, Weaver. They are a manifestation of Solara's very life force. Their light is the breath of our world. If they perish, so too will our land. And our people."

Mia explained her findings, her voice clear despite her exhaustion. "My mending techniques are designed to repair damage, to infuse life where it has been corrupted or drained. But this isn't corruption. It's an internal unraveling. The magical threads that hold the blooms together are losing their cohesion. My magic can't *re-engineer* their fundamental structure. It's like trying to rebuild a collapsing building with a needle and thread. I can patch the cracks, but I can't fix the foundation."

Ethan presented his data, the graphs and charts on his crystalline tablet showing the alarming rate of magical energy dissipation in the bloom fields. "The energy isn't being attacked or consumed," he explained, pointing to the fluctuating lines. "It's simply… leaking. As if the very fabric of reality that forms the blooms has become porous. We need to understand *why* this porosity is occurring. Why are the threads losing their cohesion?"

The elders exchanged uneasy glances. Their ancient wisdom, passed down through generations, offered no direct answers to this new, insidious threat. Their lore spoke of blights, of dark magic, of external enemies. But an internal decay, a fundamental unraveling of Solara's own magical essence, was unprecedented.

"Our prophecies speak of the Heart Weaver's ability to mend all wounds of the land," one elder, a man named Borin, his voice raspy with age, said, his gaze fixed on Mia. "Is this not a wound, Weaver?"

Mia felt the weight of their expectations, the desperate hope in their eyes. "It is a wound, yes," she replied, her voice firm. "But it is a wound I do not yet understand. My current methods are like trying to stop a flood with a teacup. I can see the problem, I can feel it, but I lack the knowledge to truly fix it. I need to understand *why* the threads are unraveling. I need to understand the fundamental *design* of Solara's magic, not just how to repair its surface."

Queen Sasha, who had been listening intently, finally spoke, her voice clear and strong, cutting through the heavy silence. "The Weaver speaks truth. This is a challenge unlike any we have faced. Malakor's darkness was a foreign invasion. This… this is a sickness from within. And if the Heart Weaver, with her unique connection to the land, cannot mend it, then we must seek a deeper understanding."

She rose from her throne, her gaze sweeping across the somber faces of her council. "Our ancient texts, our deepest lore… they speak of the **Sunken Spires**. A place of profound, ancient knowledge. A repository of the First Weavers' wisdom. It is said that within its depths lies the very blueprint of Solara's creation, the knowledge of how our world was first woven."

The mention of the Sunken Spires sent a ripple of murmurs through the council. It was a place spoken of in hushed tones, a legend, a myth, a place of immense power and forgotten dangers.

"The Sunken Spires?" Borin gasped, his eyes wide with a mixture of awe and trepidation. "But Queen, it is a place of legend! None have journeyed there in centuries! It is said to be guarded by ancient magic, by trials that test the very soul!"

"And it is said to hold the answers we seek," Queen Sasha countered, her voice unwavering. "If the Luminous Blooms are to be saved, if Solara is to endure, we must seek that knowledge. The Weaver needs the blueprints. She needs to understand the loom itself."

Mia felt a surge of both dread and exhilaration. The Sunken Spires. It sounded like something out of a fairy tale, a place of immense power and unimaginable challenges. But it also sounded like hope. The answers she needed.

"I will go," Mia declared, her voice firm. "I will go to the Sunken Spires. I will seek this knowledge."

Ethan immediately stepped forward. "And I will go with her. My instruments, my analytical mind… they might be able to help decipher whatever ancient knowledge lies there. And to help navigate whatever… trials… await."

Queen Sasha looked at them, a faint, knowing smile gracing her lips. "I expected no less, brave companions. But the journey will be perilous. The Sunken Spires lie far beyond the settled lands, in a region untouched by our people for generations. You will need guides. And preparation."

The next few days were a whirlwind of activity. Mia spent hours in her chambers, trying to understand the nature of the "unraveling." She ran her needles over various materials, from the castle's ancient stones to the vibrant sapphire leaves, trying to detect the subtle skips, the momentary voids. She found them everywhere, faint yet persistent, like a pervasive hum beneath the surface of Solara's magic. It was as if the very fabric of reality in Solara was slowly losing its integrity, its threads becoming brittle.

Her current mending techniques, designed for damage and corruption, were indeed ineffective. When she tried to reinforce a subtly flickering section of a sapphire tree, her magic, instead of binding, seemed to flow *through* it, dissipating into the surrounding air, leaving her drained and the tree no better. It was like trying to apply glue to a dissolving surface. The problem wasn't a lack of magic, but a failure of the magical structure to *hold* the magic.

Ethan, meanwhile, was preparing for the expedition. He meticulously packed his modified Earth instruments, along with several Solaraean crystalline devices designed to detect and measure magical resonance. He also packed more practical supplies: concentrated food rations, water purifiers, durable climbing gear, and a comprehensive first-aid kit. He sketched out potential routes, consulted ancient maps provided by Queen Sasha, and tried to anticipate every conceivable challenge.

"If this is a fundamental structural issue," Ethan mused one evening, poring over his notes, "then the solution won't be about adding more energy. It'll be about re-tuning. Re-aligning. Like a complex machine that's vibrating out of sync. You don't just add more power; you find the source of the vibration and fix it."

Mia nodded, her needles resting in her lap, her gaze fixed on the flickering light of a nearby luminescent crystal. "And to re-tune, I need to understand the original tuning. The blueprints of the loom."

Queen Sasha assigned them two Solaraean guides: **Elara**, the harpist whose instrument had played a jarring note, a woman of quiet strength and deep knowledge of Solaraean lore, and **Thorn**, a seasoned tracker and guardian of the sapphire forests, a stoic man with eyes that missed nothing. Both were deeply concerned about the unraveling blooms and understood the gravity of their mission.

Elara, with her artistic sensitivity, understood Mia's struggle with the subtle discord. "The land sings, Weaver," she explained gently. "And when its song falters, it is a deep pain. Your needles feel this pain, for they are attuned to the very melody of Solara." She spoke of ancient Solaraean musical theory, of harmonies and dissonances, and Mia found parallels to her own understanding of weaving and patterns.

Thorn, a man of few words, was a master of the wildlands. He knew the hidden paths, the dangers of the untamed regions, and the subtle signs of the land's health. He moved with a quiet grace, his senses constantly alert. He carried a staff carved from sapphire wood, its tip glowing faintly, a silent companion in their journey.

The departure was a solemn affair. The castle courtyard was filled with Solaraean people, their faces a mixture of hope and apprehension. Queen Sasha embraced Mia, her eyes filled with a profound trust. "Go with the light, Heart Weaver. Solara's future rests upon your needles."

Mia embraced Bean, who whimpered softly, sensing the impending separation. Hopsy, the knitted rabbit, perched on Mia's shoulder, its button eyes wide and alert, its tiny body vibrating with nervous energy. The knitted birds, usually so lively, were silent, huddled on Mia's backpack, their tiny forms almost invisible against the dark fabric.

As they rode out of the Royal City, leaving behind the shimmering castle and the worried faces of the Solaraean people, Mia looked back at the Luminous Bloom Fields. The vast expanse of flora, once a breathtaking sea of light, was now a muted, sorrowful landscape, its glow steadily dimming. The sight solidified her resolve. She had to find the answers. She had to understand the unraveling.

Their journey began through the familiar sapphire forests, now tinged with a subtle melancholy. The melodious singing was still present, but Mia could detect the faint, rhythmic skips more frequently, like a songbird briefly losing its voice. The sapphire leaves, while still vibrant, would occasionally flicker, their luminescence dimming for a fleeting moment before returning.

Thorn led the way, his movements silent and efficient, his eyes constantly scanning the dense undergrowth. Elara rode beside Mia, her expression thoughtful, occasionally humming a soft, ancient Solaraean melody that seemed to resonate with the very pulse of the land. Ethan, ever vigilant, rode at the rear, his instruments carefully packed, his mind already analyzing the challenges ahead.

They rode for days, venturing deeper into Solara's untamed wilderness. The sapphire forests gradually gave way to more rugged terrain – rolling hills covered in shimmering, iridescent grasses that swayed in the gentle breeze, resembling a vast, living tapestry. The air here was clearer, but the pervasive sense of melancholy remained, almost stronger, as if the land itself was weeping.

They encountered strange creatures – herds of graceful, multi-limbed deer with antlers that glowed faintly, and shy, furry beings that resembled oversized squirrels, their eyes like polished emeralds. Mia's knitted animals seemed to communicate with them, Hopsy twitching its nose in greeting, the knitted birds chirping in what sounded like a friendly conversation. It was a world teeming with life, but a life that seemed subdued, waiting for something to awaken it.

The subtle unraveling continued to manifest, even in these remote regions. A herd of the multi-limbed deer, usually moving with effortless grace, stumbled momentarily, their glowing antlers flickering, as if their very coordination was briefly disrupted. A patch of iridescent grass, usually shimmering with vibrant colors, momentarily turned dull and lifeless before snapping back to its usual brilliance.

Mia felt the anomalies through her needles, each flicker a tiny, unsettling void. She tried to mend them, to infuse the affected areas with restorative magic, but her efforts were futile. The magic simply flowed through, unable to bind, unable to hold. The problem was not a lack of magical energy, but a fundamental inability of the land's magical structure to retain it. It was like a sieve, slowly losing its integrity.

One evening, as they made camp in a sheltered hollow, Mia pulled out her needles, her brow furrowed in concentration. She had to understand this. She had to find a way to counter the unraveling.

"It's like the land is forgetting how to be itself," Mia murmured to Ethan, as he meticulously set up their camouflaged tent. "It's not being attacked. It's… decaying. From the inside out."

Ethan nodded, his face grim. "My readings confirm it. The magical signature of these affected areas isn't being corrupted; it's being *erased*. Temporarily. And then it re-establishes itself, but each time, it's a little weaker, a little more unstable."

He pulled out a small, crystalline device, shaped like a tuning fork. He tapped it, and it emitted a clear, resonant hum, a perfect Solaraean magical frequency. Then he held it near a patch of affected grass. The hum wavered, briefly dipping into a discordant buzz, before returning to its clear tone.

"This is a baseline resonance crystal," Ethan explained. "It's supposed to maintain a perfect magical frequency. But when it's near one of these 'unraveling' spots, it gets pulled out of tune. It's like the very fabric of space-time here is briefly losing its coherence."

Mia's eyes widened. "Space-time coherence? You think this is bigger than Solara?"

Ethan shrugged, a grim expression on his face. "I don't know. But the data suggests a fundamental instability. Something that affects the very rules of magic, not just its flow. If the magical threads are literally losing their cohesion, it implies a problem at a much deeper, more universal level than just a localized blight."

The implications were staggering. If the unraveling was a cosmic phenomenon, something that affected the very fabric of reality, how could Mia, a single Weaver, hope to stop it? Her magic, while powerful, was still rooted in Solara.

Elara, who had been listening quietly, spoke, her voice soft but clear. "Our ancient prophecies speak of the 'Great Weave,' the tapestry that binds all realms. It is said that when one thread weakens, the entire tapestry trembles. Perhaps this 'unraveling' is indeed an echo from beyond Solara, a sickness that affects the Great Weave itself."

Thorn, ever stoic, added, "The old legends also speak of the 'Heart of the World,' a place where Solara's magic is most pure, most concentrated. It is said to be the anchor of our realm, the knot that holds our threads firm. If it weakens, all of Solara weakens."

Mia felt a chill run down her spine. The Heart of the World. The Sunken Spires. Was the unraveling a symptom of a deeper problem at Solara's core? Was the Heart of the World itself losing its integrity?

The journey continued, each day bringing them closer to the uncharted territories and the legendary Sunken Spires. The landscape grew wilder, more ancient. The sapphire trees became less frequent, replaced by colossal, gnarled trees whose bark was etched with ancient, indecipherable runes. The air grew thick with a sense of immense, slumbering power, a feeling of timelessness.

The anomalies became more frequent, more intense. The melodic singing of the forest would occasionally cut out entirely, leaving an unsettling, profound silence that pressed in on them. The glowing flora would dim for longer periods, their light struggling to return. Even the ground beneath their feet would occasionally tremble with a faint, unsettling vibration, as if the very earth was sighing.

Mia's needles vibrated almost constantly now, a low, persistent thrum that echoed the land's distress. She found herself instinctively trying to weave, to mend, to bind the fleeting voids, but her magic continued to flow through, unable to grasp the dissolving threads. It was a frustrating, disheartening experience, a constant reminder of her current limitations.

One afternoon, as they traversed a narrow mountain pass, the air grew thick with a strange, shimmering haze. The light from the twin moons seemed to distort, bending unnaturally. Mia felt a sudden, sharp jolt through her needles, a profound *tear* in the magical fabric, more intense than anything she had felt before.

A section of the mountain pass directly ahead of them, a solid rock face, shimmered, then seemed to *dissolve* into a swirling vortex of shimmering, chaotic colors, revealing a glimpse of… nothingness. A void. It lasted only a few seconds, then snapped back into solid rock, leaving behind a faint, acrid smell and a profound, unsettling silence.

Bean whimpered, pressing close to Mia's leg, her fur bristling. Hopsy, the knitted rabbit, pulsed erratically, its button eyes wide with what could only be fear.

"What was that?" Ethan gasped, his face pale. His instruments were screaming, their needles violently fluctuating, unable to cope with the sudden, localized collapse of reality.

"A tear," Mia whispered, her voice trembling. "A tear in the fabric. It wasn't just a flicker. It was… a hole. A momentary hole in Solara itself."

Thorn, his stoic composure momentarily broken, stared at the spot where the void had appeared, his staff held tightly in his hand. "The Great Unraveling," he murmured, his voice filled with ancient dread. "The legends speak of it. When the threads of the Great Weave grow too thin, they tear. And the void… it hungers."

Elara's face was ashen. "It has begun. The sickness is deepening. The Sunken Spires… we must reach them quickly. Before Solara unravels completely."

The incident solidified their understanding of the threat. This was not merely a sickness; it was a fundamental instability, a slow, insidious decay that threatened to consume Solara from within. Mia's mending, designed for repair, was useless against a problem that was *dissolving* the very threads of existence. She needed more than mending; she needed to understand the **architecture of reality itself**.

They pressed on with renewed urgency, the image of the momentary void burned into their minds. The path grew more treacherous, winding through jagged, ancient mountains whose peaks pierced the bruised Solaraean sky. The air grew colder, thinner, and the silence was often broken by the unsettling *pop* of a vanishing sprite, or the mournful sigh of a dying patch of flora.

Mia spent her nights in quiet contemplation, her needles resting in her lap, trying to understand the nature of the unraveling. She tried to visualize the threads of reality, to understand how they were woven, how they were held together. Her mind struggled to grasp the abstract concept of a dissolving fabric, of a void that was not emptiness, but an absence of existence.

She tried new weaving patterns, focusing on **binding, reinforcing, creating new anchors**. She knitted a small, intricate knot from a skein of dark, resilient yarn, focusing on the concept of **stability** and **cohesion**. She imbued it with all her will, all her magic, intending it to be a miniature anchor against the unraveling.

She held the knitted knot in her hand, feeling its subtle pulse, its quiet strength. She then placed it on a patch of moss that had recently experienced a flicker. For a few minutes, the moss seemed more vibrant, its glow steadier. But then, slowly, the knot's magic began to dissipate, its threads loosening, and the moss flickered once more. The knot had provided a temporary anchor, but it could not withstand the pervasive, systemic unraveling. It was like trying to tie a knot in dissolving rope.

"It's not enough," Mia whispered to Ethan, her voice filled with frustration. "My magic can create, but it can't create a solution to this. I need to know *how* Solara was woven. What holds it together. What are the fundamental principles of its existence?"

Ethan, observing her experiments, nodded. "It's like trying to fix a complex computer program when you don't have the source code. You can see the bugs, you can even try to patch them, but without understanding the underlying logic, you can't truly fix the system."

Their journey continued, a race against time. The Sunken Spires, once a distant legend, now felt like their only hope. They were venturing into the unknown, seeking ancient knowledge that might hold the key to Solara's survival, and perhaps, the survival of other realms connected by the Great Weave. Mia's needles, though still humming with a subtle distress, were ready. Ready to learn. Ready to re-engineer. Ready to reweave the very fabric of existence. The unraveling bloom was a stark warning, a desperate plea from the land itself. And Mia, the Heart Weaver, was determined to answer.

Chapter 4: Seeking the Sunken Spires

The air, once thick with the sweet perfume of the Luminous Bloom Fields, now carried a faint, acrid tang, a scent of slow decay that clung to Mia's senses long after they had left the blighted plains behind. The image of the dying blooms, their once-vibrant colors muted to sickly rust and murky grey, was seared into her mind, a stark, heartbreaking testament to the insidious threat of the Great Unraveling. It was no longer a subtle whisper, but a desperate cry from the land, a plea that resonated with a constant, low thrum through her rosewood needles. The weight of Solara's future, of its very existence, felt heavy in her hands.

Their journey began through the familiar sapphire forests, but even here, the vibrant harmony seemed strained. The melodious singing, usually a continuous, joyful chorus, was now punctuated by increasingly frequent, unsettling silences, like a songbird briefly losing its voice mid-note. The sapphire leaves, while still shimmering with brilliance, would occasionally flicker, their luminescence dimming for a fleeting moment before snapping back, leaving a faint, unsettling void in their wake. Mia felt each of these anomalies as a tiny,

jarring tremor through her needles, a constant
reminder of the pervasive sickness.

Thorn, their stoic guide, led the way, his movements
silent and efficient, his eyes, the color of ancient
moss, constantly scanning the dense undergrowth.
He moved with an almost preternatural awareness of
the forest, his hand resting lightly on the sapphire
wood staff that glowed faintly at its tip, a silent
companion in their urgent quest. He was a man of
few words, but his presence radiated a deep
connection to the wildlands, a primal understanding
of Solara's delicate balance. His usual calm demeanor
was subtly fractured by a quiet tension, a watchful
apprehension that spoke volumes.

Elara, the harpist, rode beside Mia, her expression
thoughtful, occasionally humming a soft, ancient
Solaraean melody that seemed to resonate with the
very pulse of the land. Her artistic sensitivity made
her acutely aware of the discords Mia perceived,
even if she couldn't feel them through a weaver's
needles. She spoke of ancient Solaraean musical
theory, of harmonies and dissonances, and Mia
found profound parallels to her own understanding
of weaving and patterns. "The Great Weave," Elara
murmured one afternoon, her voice soft as the rustle
of leaves, "is like a grand symphony. Every thread,

every creature, every bloom, is a note. When a note falters, the harmony is broken. And when the very instrument itself begins to unravel, the music dies." Her words, poetic and profound, painted a vivid picture of the stakes involved.

Ethan, ever vigilant, rode at the rear, his instruments carefully packed, his mind already analyzing the challenges ahead. He meticulously logged every anomaly, every flicker, every momentary void, charting their frequency and intensity. His crystalline tablet, usually a tool for precise measurements, now often displayed chaotic, erratic readings, a testament to the unpredictable nature of the unraveling. He was trying to quantify the unquantifiable, to apply logic to a problem that defied all scientific principles. "It's like trying to measure a ghost," he'd muttered that morning, frustrated by a particularly stubborn energy spike that vanished before he could fully record it. "The moment you think you have it, it's gone."

They rode for days, venturing deeper into Solara's untamed wilderness, leaving the familiar, settled lands behind. The sapphire forests gradually gave way to more rugged terrain – rolling hills covered in shimmering, iridescent grasses that swayed in the gentle breeze, resembling a vast, living tapestry. The colors here were wilder, less cultivated, a riot of emeralds, amethysts, and golds that pulsed with an untamed energy. The air was clearer, crisper, carrying the scent of damp earth and wild, unseen blossoms. But the pervasive sense of melancholy remained, almost stronger, as if the land itself was weeping, its wild beauty tinged with a profound sadness.

They encountered strange creatures, inhabitants of these remote regions. Herds of graceful, multi-limbed deer with antlers that glowed faintly, moved with an ethereal elegance, their eyes like polished emeralds reflecting the twin moons. Shy, furry beings that resembled oversized squirrels, their tails bushy and iridescent, darted through the undergrowth, their eyes bright with curiosity. Mia's knitted animals, Hopsy and the small flock of birds, seemed to communicate with them, Hopsy twitching its nose in greeting, the knitted birds chirping in what sounded like a friendly conversation, a testament to Mia's ability to imbue her creations with a universal language of life. It was a world teeming with life, but a life that seemed subdued, waiting for something to awaken it, to restore its full vibrancy.

Yet, even in these pristine, untouched regions, the subtle unraveling continued to manifest, a creeping sickness that spared no part of Solara. A herd of the multi-limbed deer, usually moving with effortless grace, stumbled momentarily, their glowing antlers flickering, as if their very coordination was briefly disrupted by an unseen force. A patch of iridescent grass, usually shimmering with vibrant colors, momentarily turned dull and lifeless before snapping back to its usual brilliance, leaving behind a faint, acrid scent.

Mia felt the anomalies through her needles, each flicker a tiny, unsettling void, a momentary absence where magic should have been. She tried to mend them, to infuse the affected areas with restorative magic, but her efforts were futile. The magic simply flowed through, unable to bind, unable to hold. The problem was not a lack of magical energy, but a fundamental inability of the land's magical structure to retain it. It was like a sieve, slowly losing its integrity, its very substance becoming porous.

One evening, as they made camp in a sheltered hollow, the twin moons casting long, distorted shadows across the rolling hills, Mia pulled out her needles, her brow furrowed in concentration. She had to understand this. She had to find a way to counter the unraveling. She ran her fingers over a patch of moss that had just experienced a pronounced flicker, feeling the subtle tremor beneath its surface.

"It's like the land is forgetting how to be itself," Mia murmured to Ethan, as he meticulously set up their camouflaged tent, its fabric shifting to blend seamlessly with the surrounding environment. "It's not being attacked. It's… decaying. From the inside out. And my mending just… passes through it. It's like trying to knit water."

Ethan nodded, his face grim. He held a small, crystalline device, shaped like a tuning fork, near the affected moss. He tapped it, and it emitted a clear, resonant hum, a perfect Solaraean magical frequency. But when held near the unraveling spot, the hum wavered, briefly dipping into a discordant buzz, before returning to its clear tone. "My readings confirm it. The magical signature of these affected areas isn't being corrupted; it's being *erased*. Temporarily. And then it re-establishes itself, but each time, it's a little weaker, a little more unstable. This baseline resonance crystal… it's supposed to maintain a perfect magical frequency. But when it's near one of these 'unraveling' spots, it gets pulled out of tune. It's like the very fabric of space-time here is briefly losing its coherence."

Mia's eyes widened, the implications of his words washing over her like a cold wave. "Space-time coherence? You think this is bigger than Solara? You think this is affecting other realms?"

Ethan shrugged, a grim expression on his face. "I don't know. But the data suggests a fundamental instability. Something that affects the very rules of magic, not just its flow. If the magical threads are literally losing their cohesion, it implies a problem at a much deeper, more universal level than just a localized blight. It's like a flaw in the universal operating system, not just a bug in one application."

Elara, who had been listening quietly, her gaze fixed on the distant horizon, spoke, her voice soft but clear, imbued with the wisdom of generations. "Our ancient prophecies speak of the 'Great Weave,' the tapestry that binds all realms. It is said that when one thread weakens, the entire tapestry trembles. Perhaps this 'unraveling' is indeed an echo from beyond Solara, a sickness that affects the Great Weave itself. A cosmic discord."

Thorn, ever stoic, added, his voice a low rumble, "The old legends also speak of the 'Heart of the World,' a place where Solara's magic is most pure, most concentrated. It is said to be the anchor of our realm, the knot that holds our threads firm. If it weakens, all of Solara weakens. It is the core, the source of our very being."

Mia felt a chill run down her spine. The Heart of the World. The Sunken Spires. Was the unraveling a symptom of a deeper problem at Solara's core? Was the Heart of the World itself losing its integrity, its foundational threads fraying? The thought was terrifying. If Solara's anchor was weakening, then the entire realm was adrift, slowly dissolving into the void.

The journey continued, each day bringing them closer to the uncharted territories and the legendary Sunken Spires. The landscape grew wilder, more ancient, a testament to the passage of untold eons. The sapphire trees became less frequent, replaced by colossal, gnarled trees whose bark was etched with ancient, indecipherable runes that seemed to writhe and shift in the dappled light. The air grew thick with a sense of immense, slumbering power, a feeling of timelessness, as if they were stepping back into the dawn of creation. The very ground hummed with a deep, resonant vibration, a primal pulse that Mia felt through her feet, up into her bones.

The anomalies became more frequent, more intense, no longer fleeting flickers but prolonged instances of magical instability. The melodic singing of the forest would occasionally cut out entirely, leaving an unsettling, profound silence that pressed in on them, a vacuum of sound that made the air feel heavy and suffocating. The glowing flora would dim for longer periods, their light struggling to return, their petals curling inward as if in pain. Even the ground beneath their feet would occasionally tremble with a faint, unsettling vibration, as if the very earth was sighing, its ancient heart struggling to beat.

Mia's needles vibrated almost constantly now, a low, persistent thrum that echoed the land's distress. She found herself instinctively trying to weave, to mend, to bind the fleeting voids, but her magic continued to flow through, unable to grasp the dissolving threads. It was a frustrating, disheartening experience, a constant reminder of her current limitations, a profound sense of helplessness in the face of an invisible, pervasive enemy.

One afternoon, as they traversed a narrow mountain pass, the air grew thick with a strange, shimmering haze. The light from the twin moons seemed to distort, bending unnaturally, casting grotesque, elongated shadows that danced and writhed on the jagged rock faces. Mia felt a sudden, sharp jolt through her needles, a profound *tear* in the magical fabric, more intense than anything she had felt before. It was like a sudden, violent ripping sound, but without any audible noise, a purely magical sensation that sent a shockwave of cold dread through her.

A section of the mountain pass directly ahead of them, a solid rock face, shimmered, then seemed to *dissolve* into a swirling vortex of shimmering, chaotic colors, revealing a glimpse of… nothingness. A void. It was not darkness, but an absence of light, an absence of matter, an absence of existence itself. It was a terrifying glimpse into the abyss, a window into non-being. It lasted only a few seconds, then snapped back into solid rock with a faint, almost inaudible *pop*, leaving behind a faint, acrid smell, like burnt ozone, and a profound, unsettling silence that seemed to swallow all sound.

Bean whimpered, pressing close to Mia's leg, her fur bristling, her body trembling uncontrollably. Hopsy, the knitted rabbit, pulsed erratically, its button eyes wide with what could only be fear, its tiny body vibrating with an uncontrolled tremor.

"What was that?" Ethan gasped, his face pale, his eyes wide with a mixture of horror and scientific fascination. His instruments were screaming, their needles violently fluctuating, unable to cope with the sudden, localized collapse of reality. The crystalline resonance meter shattered, unable to withstand the raw, chaotic energy.

"A tear," Mia whispered, her voice trembling, barely audible. "A tear in the fabric. It wasn't just a flicker. It was… a hole. A momentary hole in Solara itself. A glimpse into the void."

Thorn, his stoic composure momentarily broken, stared at the spot where the void had appeared, his sapphire wood staff held tightly in his hand, its tip glowing with a desperate, flickering light. "The Great Unraveling," he murmured, his voice filled with ancient dread, a sound that seemed to echo from the very depths of the earth. "The legends speak of it. When the threads of the Great Weave grow too thin, they tear. And the void… it hungers. It seeks to consume all."

Elara's face was ashen, her usual calm demeanor replaced by a profound horror. "It has begun. The sickness is deepening. The Sunken Spires… we must reach them quickly. Before Solara unravels completely. Before the Great Silence claims us all." Her words, usually so melodic, were sharp with urgency, a desperate plea.

The incident solidified their understanding of the threat. This was not merely a sickness; it was a fundamental instability, a slow, insidious decay that threatened to consume Solara from within. Mia's mending, designed for repair, was useless against a problem that was *dissolving* the very threads of existence. She needed more than mending; she needed to understand the **architecture of reality itself**, the foundational principles upon which Solara, and perhaps all realms, were built.

They pressed on with renewed urgency, the image of the momentary void burned into their minds, a chilling testament to the escalating danger. The path grew more treacherous, winding through jagged, ancient mountains whose peaks pierced the bruised Solaraean sky like broken teeth. The air grew colder, thinner, biting at their exposed skin, and the silence was often broken by the unsettling *pop* of a vanishing sprite, or the mournful sigh of a dying patch of flora, their lights fading into nothingness. Even the wind seemed to carry a mournful wail, a song of sorrow from a dying land.

Mia spent her nights in quiet contemplation, her needles resting in her lap, trying to understand the nature of the unraveling. She tried to visualize the threads of reality, to understand how they were woven, how they were held together. Her mind struggled to grasp the abstract concept of a dissolving fabric, of a void that was not emptiness, but an absence of existence. She felt the pervasive weakness, the subtle decay, in every fiber of her being, a constant, low hum of distress from Solara itself.

She tried new weaving patterns, focusing on **binding, reinforcing, creating new anchors**. She knitted a small, intricate knot from a skein of dark, resilient yarn, focusing on the concept of **stability** and **cohesion**. She imbued it with all her will, all her magic, intending it to be a miniature anchor against the unraveling. She held the knitted knot in her hand, feeling its subtle pulse, its quiet strength. She then placed it on a patch of moss that had recently experienced a flicker. For a few minutes, the moss seemed more vibrant, its glow steadier. But then, slowly, inexorably, the knot's magic began to dissipate, its threads loosening, and the moss flickered once more. The knot had provided a temporary anchor, but it could not withstand the pervasive, systemic unraveling. It was like trying to tie a knot in dissolving rope, a futile gesture against a fundamental flaw.

"It's not enough," Mia whispered to Ethan, her voice filled with frustration, a profound sense of helplessness creeping into her heart. "My magic can create, but it can't create a solution to this. I need to know *how* Solara was woven. What holds it together. What are the fundamental principles of its existence? It's like trying to fix a complex computer program when you don't have the source code. You can see the bugs, you can even try to patch them, but without understanding the underlying logic, you can't truly fix the system."

Ethan, observing her experiments, nodded, his own face etched with worry. "You're right. We need the original schematics. The foundational algorithms. The blueprints of the loom itself." He pulled out his battered journal, flipping through pages filled with complex equations and diagrams. "My instruments are useless against this kind of instability. They can only tell us *what* is happening, not *why*."

Their journey led them through the **Whispering Canyons**, a series of deep, winding gorges carved by ancient, unseen forces. The walls of the canyons were sheer, towering cliffs of dark, crystalline rock, scarred with millennia of erosion. The air here was colder, and the wind, funneled through the narrow passages, created an eerie, mournful wail, a sound that seemed to carry the sorrows of ages. The ground was uneven, strewn with jagged shards of luminous crystal that glittered faintly in the dim light, casting dancing shadows that seemed to writhe with a life of their own.

The unraveling manifested differently here. Instead of momentary voids, they encountered **localized distortions in time and space**. A section of the canyon wall would suddenly shimmer, and for a fleeting moment, they would see a glimpse of another era – ancient Solaraean warriors marching through the pass, or colossal, glowing beasts grazing on long-extinct flora. The images would flicker, then vanish, leaving behind a faint, metallic scent and a profound sense of disorientation.

"Temporal echoes," Ethan murmured, his eyes wide with scientific awe, even as his body trembled from the unsettling sensation. "The fabric of reality isn't just tearing; it's becoming thin enough to let past and future bleed through. It's like the universe is having a bad dream."

Mia felt these temporal echoes through her needles, a dizzying swirl of conflicting energies, a cacophony of past and present that left her feeling nauseous and disoriented. Her magic, usually so responsive, felt sluggish, unable to grasp the fleeting, ephemeral nature of these distortions.

Thorn, however, seemed to navigate the canyons with an almost uncanny ease. He would pause, his head cocked, listening to the subtle shifts in the wind, then point to a specific path, guiding them around the most unstable areas. "The land remembers," he said, his voice a low rumble. "Even when it falters, its memory remains. We follow the ancient currents."

Elara, too, found a way to cope. She would hum soft, intricate melodies, ancient Solaraean songs that seemed to resonate with the temporal distortions, subtly stabilizing the air around them, making the echoes less jarring. Her music was a balm against the chaos, a reminder of Solara's inherent harmony.

They faced other challenges. The canyons were home to **Shadow Stalkers**, elusive creatures of pure shadow, drawn to areas of magical instability. They were not malicious, but opportunistic, feeding on the fleeting voids and the temporal echoes. They moved like wraiths, barely visible against the dark canyon walls, their eyes glowing with a cold, predatory light.

One evening, as they made camp in a small, sheltered alcove, a Shadow Stalker detached itself from the gloom, its form coalescing into a gaunt, predatory shape. It moved silently, its glowing eyes fixed on Bean, who whimpered, pressing close to Mia's leg.

Mia's needles, though still humming with distress, pulsed with a sudden surge of protective energy. She couldn't fight it directly, but she could deter it. She pulled out a skein of shimmering, iridescent yarn, focusing on **distraction, overwhelming light, sensory overload**.

She knitted a flurry of tiny, glowing sprites, imbued with a chaotic, dazzling energy. She flung them towards the Shadow Stalker. The sprites exploded into a blinding burst of light, swirling around the creature, their tiny forms flashing with every color of the rainbow. The air filled with a cacophony of joyful chirps and melodic singing, a dazzling, overwhelming assault on the creature's senses.

The Shadow Stalker shrieked, a sound of pure frustration and pain. It recoiled, its smoky form flickering, unable to withstand the pure, vibrant light. It dissolved back into the shadows, its glowing eyes fading into the gloom.

"That was amazing, Mia!" Ethan exclaimed, breathless. "You literally blinded it with science… and knitting!"

Mia, panting, felt the drain on her energy, but a surge of triumph filled her. Her magic, though unable to mend the unraveling, could still protect. It could still create. It could still bring light into the encroaching darkness.

As they ventured deeper into the canyons, the air grew colder, and the wind's mournful wail intensified. The luminous crystals on the ground became more frequent, larger, their internal light pulsing with an erratic, almost frantic beat. They were nearing the heart of the instability.

One morning, they stumbled upon a colossal, ancient structure, half-buried in the canyon floor. It was a massive, circular stone platform, its surface etched with intricate, indecipherable runes that glowed faintly. In its center, a single, towering monolith of dark, crystalline rock pierced the sky, its surface shimmering with a faint, iridescent haze.

"The **Resonance Stone**," Elara whispered, her voice filled with reverence. "An ancient Solaraean artifact. It is said to anchor the magical currents of this region, to stabilize the Great Weave."

Ethan immediately pulled out his instruments. His remaining crystalline devices, though battered, still functioned. He ran a scanner over the Resonance Stone. The readings were chaotic, a violent storm of fluctuating energies. "It's… it's completely out of sync," he murmured, his face grim. "Its resonance is failing. It's not anchoring anything. It's contributing to the instability."

Mia knelt, her hand resting on the Resonance Stone. Her needles vibrated fiercely, a frantic, desperate thrum. She felt the stone's profound distress, its struggle to maintain its purpose against the overwhelming force of the unraveling. It was like a dying heart, struggling to beat.

"Can you fix it, Mia?" Ethan asked, his voice filled with a desperate hope.

Mia closed her eyes, focusing all her will, all her magic, on the Resonance Stone. She chose a skein of pure, vibrant gold yarn, the color of Solara's purest light. She began to knit, not a physical object, but a **pattern of pure resonance**, a complex, intricate weave of energy that mirrored the stone's original, perfect frequency. She poured her essence into the stitches, willing the stone to remember its harmony, to re-tune itself.

As she knitted, the golden yarn seemed to melt into the stone, becoming one with its essence. The runes on the stone's surface began to glow, faintly at first, then with increasing brilliance. The erratic fluctuations on Ethan's instruments began to stabilize, the chaotic lines smoothing into a steady, rhythmic pulse. The air around them grew warmer, filled with a profound sense of peace.

The Resonance Stone began to hum, a low, resonant thrum that vibrated through the canyon, echoing through the very earth. It was a sound of deep, ancient harmony, a perfect note in Solara's symphony. The shimmering haze in the air dissipated, the temporal echoes vanished, and the wind's mournful wail softened to a gentle sigh.

Mia, panting, leaned back, her energy completely depleted. Her needles were cold, lifeless, their warmth completely gone. She had pushed herself to her absolute limit, channeling every ounce of her magic into the Resonance Stone.

"It worked," Ethan breathed, his voice filled with awe. His instruments now showed a perfect, stable resonance emanating from the stone. "You re-tuned it, Mia! You literally re-tuned the fabric of reality!"

Elara and Thorn knelt before Mia, their faces filled with reverence. "The Heart Weaver," Elara whispered, tears shining in her eyes. "You have brought harmony back to this place. You have shown us the path."

Mia managed a weak smile. The Resonance Stone was stable, but the unraveling was still a pervasive threat. She had temporarily mended a symptom, but not cured the disease. She still needed the blueprints.

They rested at the Resonance Stone, allowing its newly restored harmony to replenish their spirits. Mia's needles, though still cold, felt a faint, returning warmth, a subtle promise of renewed power.

As they continued their journey, the landscape began to change once more. The jagged mountains gave way to a vast, shimmering plain, its surface covered in a fine, iridescent dust that sparkled with every color of the rainbow. The air here was still and silent, filled with a profound sense of anticipation.

"We are close," Thorn murmured, his eyes fixed on the distant horizon. "The Sunken Spires… they lie beyond this plain. Hidden beneath the shimmering dust."

Elara added, "The legends say the Spires are not built, but grown. Formed from the very essence of Solara's creation, a living repository of ancient knowledge."

Mia felt a thrill of excitement, mingled with a lingering apprehension. The Sunken Spires. The place that held the answers. The blueprints of the loom. She looked at her needles, now faintly warm in her hand, ready for whatever knowledge awaited her.

Their journey was nearing its end, but the greatest challenge, the true reweaving of Solara, was yet to come. The unraveling bloom was a stark warning, a desperate plea from the land itself. And Mia, the Heart Weaver, was determined to answer, to understand, and to reweave the very fabric of existence.

Chapter 5: Trials of the Verdant Maze

The shimmering plain stretched before them, a vast, silent expanse of iridescent dust that sparkled with every color of the rainbow under the twin moons. The air here was still, almost heavy with anticipation, a profound quiet that seemed to hum with unseen energy. It was a stark contrast to the mournful wail of the Whispering Canyons they had just left, a silence that felt less like peace and more like a held breath. Thorn had called it the **"Veil of Anticipation,"** the final threshold before the Sunken Spires.

Mia's needles, now faintly warm in her hand, pulsed with a subtle, insistent thrum, a mixture of apprehension and excitement. The temporary re-tuning of the Resonance Stone had replenished her magic, but the memory of the unraveling bloom and the momentary void in the mountain pass still lingered, a chilling reminder of the pervasive threat. She looked at Ethan, his face etched with a mixture of weariness and grim determination, and then at Elara and Thorn, their Solaraean faces reflecting the solemnity of their quest. Bean, nestled close to Mia's leg, whimpered softly, sensing the shift in the air, while Hopsy, perched on Mia's shoulder, twitched its nose, its button eyes wide with alert curiosity.

"The Spires are hidden beneath this plain," Thorn murmured, his voice a low rumble that seemed to vibrate with the very ground. "They reveal themselves only to those who are truly sought, and truly seek. The legends say the path is not found, but *woven*." He swept a hand across the shimmering dust.

As they stepped onto the plain, the iridescent dust swirled around their boots, rising in faint, sparkling clouds that seemed to catch the moonlight and hold it. With every step, Mia felt a subtle shift in the magical currents beneath her feet, a complex, intricate pattern of energy that seemed to pulse and flow with a deliberate, almost sentient rhythm. It was as if the ground itself was alive, a vast, slumbering consciousness.

They walked for hours, the plain stretching endlessly before them, the twin moons slowly traversing the sky. The air grew thicker, heavier, imbued with an ancient, profound magic that pressed in on them from all sides. The silence deepened, becoming almost absolute, broken only by the soft crunch of their boots on the iridescent dust and the rhythmic thrum of Mia's needles.

Then, as the primary moon began its slow descent, painting the horizon in bruised purples and grays, the plain began to shimmer. Not with the gentle sparkle of the dust, but with a profound, internal luminescence. The ground beneath them began to undulate, slowly at first, then with increasing intensity, like a vast, living ocean.

From the shimmering dust, colossal structures began to rise. Not towers of stone or metal, but immense, spiraling forms of living, glowing flora. Vines as thick as ancient trees twisted upwards, their leaves a vibrant, pulsing emerald, forming towering walls that stretched to the bruised sky. Flowers the size of small homes bloomed in impossible colors – incandescent blues, fiery oranges, deep, shimmering violets – their petals unfurling in slow, deliberate movements, revealing intricate, glowing patterns within. The air filled with a sweet, intoxicating perfume, mingled with the earthy scent of damp soil and the metallic tang of raw magic.

The structures grew, intertwining and connecting, forming a vast, intricate network of living walls, archways, and spiraling pathways. It was a place of breathtaking beauty, yet tinged with an undeniable sense of being watched, of being *tested*. This was not a natural formation; it was a deliberate creation, a living puzzle.

"The **Verdant Maze**," Elara whispered, her voice filled with awe and a hint of trepidation. "The gateway to the Sunken Spires. It is said to be a living test, woven by the First Weavers to guard their knowledge."

Mia's needles vibrated fiercely, a frantic, excited thrum. She felt the immense, complex weave of the maze, a tapestry of living magic that pulsed with a profound, intricate energy. It was unlike anything she had ever encountered, a magical structure that was constantly shifting, growing, and adapting.

"It's… alive," Ethan breathed, his eyes wide with a mixture of scientific fascination and profound wonder. He pulled out his instruments, but they immediately went haywire, their needles spinning wildly, unable to cope with the sheer density and complexity of the magical energy emanating from the maze. "My instruments are useless here. It's too much. The magic is too… organic."

Thorn, his face grim, drew his sapphire wood staff. "The maze tests more than strength. It tests spirit. It tests resolve. And it tests the Weaver." His gaze met Mia's, a silent challenge.

They approached the entrance, a massive archway formed by two intertwining, glowing vines. The air here was thick with the maze's perfume, almost dizzying in its intensity. As they stepped through, the archway shimmered, then closed behind them with a soft *thump*, sealing them within the living labyrinth.

The interior of the Verdant Maze was a world unto itself. Pathways of glowing moss wound through towering walls of living flora, their leaves forming a dense canopy that filtered the twin moons' light into dappled, ethereal patterns. The air was filled with the soft rustle of growing vines, the gentle hum of unseen insects, and the constant, rhythmic pulse of the maze's living magic. It was beautiful, but also profoundly disorienting. The pathways twisted and turned, seemingly without logic, leading them deeper into the labyrinth's embrace.

Mia's first instinct was to try her usual weaving methods. She focused on creating a clear, stable path, a thread of direction through the confusion. She chose a skein of bright, guiding light yarn, intending to weave a luminous trail that would lead them forward. But as she began to knit, her needles encountered an unexpected resistance. The maze's own magic, vast and intricate, seemed to absorb her threads, twisting them, distorting their intended purpose. The luminous trail she tried to weave would flicker, then bend abruptly, leading them in circles, or simply vanishing into the living walls.

The unraveling, too, manifested differently here. Instead of momentary voids, the maze itself would subtly *shift*. A pathway they had just taken would suddenly be gone, replaced by a dense wall of vines. A familiar landmark – a particularly large, glowing bloom, or a uniquely twisted vine – would momentarily shimmer, then change its form, its color, its very essence, before snapping back, leaving them disoriented and questioning their own perceptions. It was as if the maze was actively trying to confuse them, to break their sense of reality.

"It's like the maze is alive, and it's playing games with us," Ethan muttered, frustrated, after they had walked in a circle for the third time. He tried to map their progress on his crystalline tablet, but the maze's constant shifts rendered his efforts futile. "Every time I think I have a pattern, it changes. The spatial dimensions are… fluid."

Elara, however, found her own way to navigate the chaos. She would close her eyes, her fingers brushing the glowing leaves of the maze, and hum soft, intricate melodies. Her music seemed to resonate with the maze's living magic, detecting subtle currents, faint harmonies that indicated a true path, or a momentary weakness in an illusory wall. "The maze has a song, Weaver," she explained, her voice soft. "A complex, ever-changing melody. When it is in harmony, it guides. When it is discordant, it misleads. We must listen to its true rhythm."

Thorn, ever reliant on instinct, moved with a quiet, almost primal awareness. He would pause, his head cocked, listening to the subtle rustle of the vines, the faint scent of the air, the almost imperceptible shift in the ground beneath his feet. He seemed to sense the "true" path even when it was hidden by illusion, his connection to the wildlands guiding him through the living labyrinth. "The maze tries to confuse the mind," he rumbled, his eyes scanning the shifting walls. "But the land speaks to the spirit. We follow the whispers of the roots."

Their first major trial came as they encountered a section of the maze where the pathways were entirely illusory. They seemed to stretch endlessly before them, shimmering with inviting light, but when they tried to step onto them, their feet would pass through, revealing a dizzying drop into a chasm of swirling, chaotic colors.

"It's a trap," Ethan stated, peering into the illusory abyss. "A magical illusion designed to make us fall."

Mia's needles vibrated with a desperate urgency. Her mending magic was useless here. She couldn't mend an illusion. She needed to create something real, something tangible, to anchor their perception. She pulled out a skein of thick, resilient yarn, focusing on **solidity, stability, anchoring**. She began to knit a series of small, circular platforms, imbued with the power to temporarily solidify the illusory pathways.

As she knitted, she flung the platforms onto the shimmering path. They landed with a soft *thump*, instantly solidifying the illusion, creating temporary, stable stepping stones across the chasm. The platforms glowed faintly, their solid forms a stark contrast to the swirling chaos beneath.

"Quickly!" Mia urged, panting from the effort of maintaining the platforms. "They won't last long!"

They leaped from platform to platform, their feet finding solid ground where moments before there had been only air. Bean, surprisingly agile, followed Mia, her paws finding purchase on the glowing discs. Hopsy, the knitted rabbit, pulsed with a faint, inner light, its button eyes wide with excitement. They made it across, breathless but triumphant, just as the last platform dissolved back into the shimmering illusion.

Their next challenge was a section of the maze filled with **Memory Weaves**. Here, the living walls of the labyrinth would shimmer, and projections of past events would play out before them – ancient Solaraean battles, joyous celebrations, moments of profound sorrow. The images were so vivid, so real, that they threatened to overwhelm their senses, pulling them into the past, disorienting them, trying to make them lose their way.

Mia felt a dizzying swirl of conflicting emotions through her needles, a cacophony of past and present that left her feeling nauseous and disoriented. Her magic, usually so responsive, felt sluggish, unable to grasp the fleeting, ephemeral nature of these distortions. The unraveling manifested here as moments where the memories would become distorted, fragmented, or even merge with their own, creating a terrifying confusion.

Elara stepped forward, her face serene despite the swirling chaos. She closed her eyes, and began to hum a soft, intricate melody, an ancient Solaraean song that seemed to resonate with the temporal distortions. Her music was a balm against the chaos, a reminder of Solara's inherent harmony. As she hummed, the memories softened, becoming less intrusive, less overwhelming. The discordant fragments of the past seemed to coalesce, becoming clearer, more coherent, allowing them to observe without being consumed.

"The song of harmony," Elara explained, her voice a gentle murmur. "It reminds the weave of its true purpose, its true rhythm. It filters the discord."

They moved through the Memory Weaves, guided by Elara's soothing melody, their minds protected from the overwhelming influx of the past. It was a slow, meditative process, a journey through Solara's history, glimpsing moments of its glory and its pain.

As they ventured deeper into the maze, the living walls grew denser, more complex, and the unraveling became more intense. The pathways would not just shift, but entire sections of the maze would momentarily *dissolve* into the void, leaving gaping holes that snapped back into existence with a terrifying *pop*. The melodic hum of the maze would occasionally cut out entirely, leaving an unsettling, profound silence that pressed in on them, a vacuum of sound that made the air feel heavy and suffocating.

Mia's needles vibrated almost constantly now, a low, persistent thrum that echoed the maze's distress. She found herself instinctively trying to weave, to mend, to bind the fleeting voids, but her magic continued to flow through, unable to grasp the dissolving threads. It was a frustrating, disheartening experience, a constant reminder of her current limitations, a profound sense of helplessness in the face of an invisible, pervasive enemy.

"It's like the maze itself is unraveling," Ethan observed, his voice grim, as a section of a glowing vine wall momentarily vanished, revealing a glimpse of the void beyond. "It's fighting against its own existence."

Their next trial involved **Living Barriers**. These were sections where the maze's vines would grow at an accelerated, aggressive rate, twisting into dense, impenetrable thickets that blocked their path, or ensnared them in their thorny embrace. These were not mere plants; they were imbued with a malevolent, binding magic, designed to trap and hold.

Mia tried to cut through them with a magically sharpened knitted blade, but the vines would immediately regrow, their thorny branches lashing out. Her usual mending magic, designed to infuse life, only seemed to make them grow faster, stronger.

"My magic is making it worse!" Mia exclaimed, frustrated. "It's like they're feeding on it!"

Thorn stepped forward, his eyes narrowed. He raised his sapphire wood staff, and a faint, emerald light pulsed from its tip. He began to trace intricate patterns in the air, movements that seemed to resonate with the maze's own growth. The vines, instead of growing, began to subtly *recede*, their thorny branches twisting inward, creating a narrow, winding passage.

"These vines are woven with the maze's life force," Thorn explained, his voice a low rumble. "They cannot be fought with force, or with life-giving magic. They must be persuaded. They must be *unwoven* from within." He demonstrated, carefully guiding the vines with his staff, subtly redirecting their growth, creating a path where moments before there had been an impenetrable barrier.

Mia watched, fascinated. Thorn wasn't fighting the maze; he was *negotiating* with it. He was understanding its internal logic, its inherent patterns of growth, and subtly redirecting them. It was a form of weaving, but one she hadn't yet mastered — the art of weaving *through* existing magical structures, not just creating new ones.

She pulled out a skein of fine, almost invisible yarn, focusing on **redirection, subtle influence, internal unwinding**. She began to knit, mirroring Thorn's movements, trying to understand the intricate patterns of growth and recession. As she knitted, her threads seemed to merge with the vines, subtly influencing their direction, creating small, temporary openings that allowed them to pass. It was slow, painstaking work, requiring immense precision and a deep understanding of the maze's living weave.

They navigated the Living Barriers, Mia and Thorn working in tandem, Mia's magic subtly influencing the vines, Thorn's ancient knowledge guiding their movements. It was a dance of influence, a delicate negotiation with the maze's living essence.

As they progressed, they encountered **Magical Traps and Guardians**. These were not physical obstacles, but subtle magical constructs, woven into the very fabric of the maze, designed to test their combined skills. One trap manifested as a sudden, overwhelming illusion of a familiar place – Newark, Arkansas, their quiet home, complete with the scent of cedar and the sound of distant traffic. It was designed to disorient, to make them question their reality, to make them long for escape.

Mia felt a powerful pull towards the illusion, a sudden, aching longing for the mundane comforts of Earth. Her needles vibrated with a desperate yearning, trying to weave her back to that familiar reality.

Ethan immediately recognized the danger. "It's a psychological trap, Mia! It's trying to make you lose focus, to make you doubt your purpose!" He grabbed her hand, his touch a grounding force. "It's not real, Mia. Focus on Solara. Focus on the maze."

Elara began to hum, a sharp, discordant melody that grated against the illusion, breaking its soothing spell. Thorn, meanwhile, used his staff to tap the ground, creating a series of rhythmic thumps that resonated with the maze's true pulse, cutting through the illusory sounds.

Mia, with their combined help, focused her will. She pulled out a skein of shimmering, iridescent yarn, focusing on **clarity, truth, illusion breaking**. She knitted a small, intricate pattern, a **"Truth Knot,"** and flung it into the heart of the illusion. The knot exploded in a burst of pure, white light, shattering the illusion of Newark, revealing the twisting, living walls of the Verdant Maze once more. The air cleared, and the longing faded, replaced by a renewed sense of purpose.

They also encountered small, elusive **Maze Guardians**, creatures woven from the maze's own essence, resembling miniature, glowing gargoyles.

They were not powerful, but they were swift and numerous, designed to harass and distract, to wear down their resolve.

Mia used her knitted birds, imbued with extra speed and agility, to distract the guardians, drawing their attention away. Ethan used his remaining crystalline devices, now carefully recalibrated, to emit high-frequency magical pulses that disoriented the creatures. Thorn, with surprising speed, would use his staff to swat them away, his movements precise and efficient. It was a constant, tiring battle of attrition, a test of their combined endurance.

As they pushed deeper into the labyrinth, the unraveling became more intense, more pervasive. The momentary voids became more frequent, lasting longer, threatening to collapse entire sections of the maze. The melodic hum of the maze would cut out entirely, leaving prolonged periods of unsettling silence. The glowing flora would dim to near-nothingness, their light struggling to return. The very ground beneath their feet would occasionally tremble violently, as if the maze itself was in agony.

Mia's needles vibrated almost constantly now, a frantic, desperate thrum that echoed the maze's profound distress. She felt the pervasive weakness, the subtle decay, in every fiber of her being, a constant, low hum of distress from Solara itself. Her magic, though replenished by the Resonance Stone, felt increasingly ineffective against the sheer scale of the unraveling. She could create, she could mend, she could protect, but she could not stop the fundamental decay.

It was during one such moment, as a large section of the maze wall ahead of them briefly dissolved into a gaping void, that Mia had a breakthrough. She had been trying to fight the unraveling, to mend it, to bind it. But what if she needed to understand it? To weave *with* it?

She closed her eyes, letting her senses expand, embracing the chaotic energies of the maze, the subtle shifts, the fleeting voids. She felt the intricate patterns of its growth, its constant, organic flux. And then she felt the unraveling, not as a destructive force, but as a *process*. A natural, albeit accelerated, process of deconstruction. It was like watching a complex piece of knitting slowly come undone, stitch by stitch.

Her needles, which had been vibrating frantically, suddenly settled into a new, rhythmic pulse, a deeper, more profound hum. She realized the maze wasn't just a physical structure; it was a complex **magical weave itself**. A living tapestry, constantly being woven and unwoven by its own inherent magic. The unraveling was not an external attack, but a malfunction in its own internal weaving process.

Mia pulled out a skein of shimmering, almost translucent silver yarn, the kind she used for her most ethereal creations. But this time, she focused not on creation, but on **deconstruction, understanding, mirroring**. She began to knit, not a new object, but a **"Mirror Weave,"** a pattern that mirrored the maze's own unraveling process, but in reverse. She was learning to *unweave* in a controlled, constructive way, to understand the precise point where the threads lost their cohesion.

As she knitted, the silver yarn seemed to merge with the maze's essence. The section of the maze wall that had dissolved before them began to subtly *re-weave* itself, its threads coalescing, its form solidifying with a newfound stability. It was not a mending, but a re-integration, a subtle recalibration of its own internal weave.

"It's stabilizing!" Ethan exclaimed, his eyes wide with awe, as his instruments showed a sudden, dramatic improvement in the magical resonance of the maze section. "The energy isn't leaking anymore! It's… flowing back in!"

Mia, panting, felt a profound sense of understanding. She wasn't just mending; she was learning to *re-engineer* the weave itself. She was learning to speak the maze's own language, to understand its fundamental architecture. This was the blueprint. This was the knowledge she needed to save the Luminous Blooms, to save Solara.

They continued their journey, Mia now weaving with a newfound confidence. She would sense an area of instability, a section where the unraveling was most pronounced, and then, using her Mirror Weave, she would subtly re-integrate its threads, stabilizing its structure, allowing them to pass safely. It was a delicate, intricate dance, a profound collaboration with the living maze.

Finally, after what felt like an eternity, the living walls began to thin. The pathways widened, and the air grew lighter, filled with a profound sense of ancient power. They had reached the heart of the maze.

They emerged into a vast, circular chamber, open to the sky, where the twin moons shone with an almost blinding brilliance. In the center of the chamber, a colossal, spiraling structure of living, glowing vines reached towards the heavens, its tendrils intertwining to form a massive, intricate **"Loom of Creation."** Its threads, shimmering with every color of the rainbow, pulsed with an immense, benevolent energy, a profound sense of ancient harmony. This was the true Heart of the Maze, the very core of its being, the source of its constant weaving.

But the Loom of Creation was not perfect. A single, massive thread, glowing with a dull, sickly grey, was slowly unraveling from its center, its fibers dissolving into nothingness. It was the source of the maze's instability, the core of its internal decay. And as it unraveled, the entire Loom trembled, its vibrant colors dimming, its harmonious hum faltering.

"The source," Elara whispered, her voice filled with a profound sadness. "The heart of the maze itself is unraveling."

Suddenly, from the shadows of the Loom, a figure emerged. Not a creature of darkness, but a being woven from the maze's own essence, a colossal, humanoid figure formed from intertwining vines and glowing flora. Its eyes, like polished emeralds, held an ancient wisdom, but also a profound sorrow. It was the **Guardian of the Loom**, a living embodiment of the maze's purpose, its final test.

"You have come far, Weaver," the Guardian rumbled, its voice a deep, resonant hum that vibrated through the chamber. "You have learned to weave with the maze, to understand its patterns. But can you mend the un-mendable? Can you reweave the thread of its very being?" Its gaze fixed on Mia, a silent challenge.

Mia looked at the unraveling thread, then at her needles, now humming with a profound, resonant warmth. She understood. This was the ultimate test. Not just to mend, but to reweave a foundational thread, to understand the very process of unraveling and to reverse it. This was the blueprint.

"I will try," Mia declared, her voice clear and strong, resonating with a newfound confidence.

She pulled out a skein of shimmering, iridescent yarn, the kind she had used for her Mirror Weave, but this time, she focused on **reconstruction, re-integration, ultimate harmony**. She approached the Loom of Creation, her needles poised. She began to knit, not just on the unraveling thread, but on the very essence of the Loom itself, weaving a new pattern of profound stability, a blueprint for its enduring harmony.

As she knitted, the iridescent yarn seemed to merge with the Loom, becoming one with its essence. The dull, sickly grey thread began to shimmer, its fibers coalescing, re-forming, slowly re-integrating into the vibrant tapestry of the Loom. The Loom of Creation hummed with a renewed intensity, its colors brightening, its harmonious song swelling, filling the chamber with a profound sense of peace and vitality.

Mia poured every ounce of her magic, every fiber of her being, into the weaving. It was a monumental task, a profound act of creation that went beyond simple mending. She was reweaving the very fabric of existence, understanding the intricate dance of creation and deconstruction.

Finally, with a last, powerful surge of magic, Mia tied off the last knot. The unraveling thread was gone, completely re-integrated into the Loom of Creation. The Loom pulsed with a brilliant, blinding light, its harmony restored, its song a triumphant symphony that resonated through the entire Verdant Maze.

The Guardian of the Loom bowed its massive head, its emerald eyes shining with profound gratitude. "You have succeeded, Heart Weaver. You have learned the weave of creation. The blueprints are yours. The Sunken Spires await."

Mia, panting, leaned back, her energy completely depleted, but a profound sense of accomplishment filling her. Her needles, though cold and lifeless, had performed the impossible. She had not just mended; she had rewoven.

The walls of the Verdant Maze around them began to shimmer, then slowly, gracefully, to recede, dissolving into swirling patterns of light and color. The living flora softened, its vibrant hues becoming less intense, its intricate patterns simplifying. The maze was opening, revealing the path forward.

They emerged from the Verdant Maze onto a vast, open plain, bathed in the soft, ethereal glow of the twin moons. Before them, half-buried beneath a shimmering layer of iridescent dust, rose the **Sunken Spires**. Not built, but grown, their forms spiraling upwards like colossal, crystalline plants, pulsing with a soft, internal light. They were a testament to ancient knowledge, a repository of the First Weavers' wisdom.

Mia looked at Ethan, her face streaked with dirt and exhaustion, but her eyes shining with a fierce determination. She had faced the unraveling, she had learned its language, and she had rewoven a piece of Solara's very essence. The blueprints of the loom, the knowledge to save Solara, awaited them. Their journey was far from over, but they had taken a monumental step. The unraveling bloom was a stark warning, but Mia, the Heart Weaver, had found the key to its reweaving. The Sunken Spires beckoned.

Chapter 6: Seeking the Sunken Spires

The air on the vast, open plain was thick with the scent of ancient dust and a profound, almost overwhelming sense of anticipation. Before them, half-buried beneath a shimmering layer of iridescent dust, rose the **Sunken Spires**. They were not built, but grown, their forms spiraling upwards like colossal, crystalline plants, pulsing with a soft, internal light that seemed to breathe with the rhythm of the twin moons. Their surfaces, smooth and translucent, shimmered with every color of the rainbow, reflecting the ethereal glow of the Solaraean sky. They were a testament to ancient knowledge, a repository of the First Weavers' wisdom, and a beacon of hope against the encroaching unraveling.

Mia's needles, though still cool and lifeless from the monumental effort of reweaving the Loom of Creation in the Verdant Maze, thrummed with a faint, sympathetic vibration. She felt the immense, benevolent energy emanating from the Spires, a profound sense of ancient harmony that resonated deep within her soul. It was a stark contrast to the chaotic, unsettling pulse of the unraveling that still permeated Solara.

Ethan stood beside her, his face streaked with dirt and exhaustion, but his eyes wide with a mixture of scientific awe and profound wonder. He pulled out his battered crystalline tablet, its screen still flickering from the maze's chaotic energies, and tried to take a reading. The device immediately went silent, its lights dimming, as if overwhelmed by the sheer density of magic in the air. "Well," he breathed, a wry grin touching his lips, "I guess my instruments are officially useless here. This place… it's beyond anything I've ever encountered."

Elara, her face serene, stepped forward, her fingers brushing the shimmering dust that covered the plain. "The Spires are not merely structures, companions," she murmured, her voice filled with reverence. "They are living conduits of Solara's oldest magic. They do not merely *hold* knowledge; they *are* knowledge. Woven from the very essence of creation by the First Weavers themselves."

Thorn, ever stoic, drew his sapphire wood staff, its tip glowing with a steady, emerald light. "The legends say the Spires guard their secrets fiercely. They test the spirit, the mind, and the very essence of those who seek their wisdom. Be vigilant. Not all trials are physical." His gaze swept across the towering, crystalline forms, his eyes missing nothing.

They approached the nearest Spire, a colossal, spiraling column that seemed to pulse with an inner light. Its surface was smooth, almost liquid, and as they drew closer, Mia could see intricate, swirling patterns etched into its crystalline skin – not carvings, but organic formations, like the growth rings of an impossibly ancient tree. They were patterns of energy, of magic, of creation itself.

As Mia reached out to touch the Spire, her needles, still nestled in her knitting bag, suddenly flared with a brilliant, golden light. A warmth spread through her hand, up her arm, and into her very being, a profound surge of energy that revitalized her, replenishing her magic to an unprecedented degree. Her needles hummed with a triumphant, resonant thrum, vibrating with boundless power. She felt completely restored, stronger than ever before, her senses heightened, her connection to the Great Weave more profound.

"My magic!" Mia gasped, her eyes wide with wonder. "It's… it's fully restored! And more! It feels… boundless!"

Ethan, watching, felt a similar surge of energy, a profound sense of peace and clarity. Elara and Thorn, too, seemed to draw strength from the Spires, their faces softening, their weariness fading.

"The Spires recognize the Heart Weaver," Elara whispered, tears shining in her eyes. "They offer their strength to those who seek to mend Solara. You are truly attuned, Weaver."

They realized the Spires were not just a destination, but a source of power, a place where Mia could draw upon the ancient magic of Solara, replenishing her reserves and deepening her understanding of her own abilities. This was vital. The unraveling was still a pervasive threat, and she would need every ounce of power to face it.

They found an entrance to the Spires, not a grand archway, but a subtle seam in the crystalline surface, a swirling vortex of light that beckoned them inward. As they stepped through, the air grew thick with a profound, ancient silence, broken only by the soft, rhythmic pulse of the Spires' internal light.

The interior of the Sunken Spires was unlike anything they had ever imagined. It was not a series of rooms or corridors, but a vast, spiraling chamber that seemed to stretch endlessly upwards, its walls formed from massive, translucent crystals that glowed with a soft, internal luminescence. Pathways of shimmering light wound through the chamber, leading upwards into the ethereal gloom. The air was cool, clean, and filled with a faint, sweet scent, like pure light distilled into perfume.

And everywhere, etched into the crystalline walls, floating in shimmering projections of light, or subtly woven into the very fabric of the pathways, were **patterns**. Intricate, swirling, mesmerizing patterns of light and energy. They were not static images, but living, dynamic formations, constantly shifting, flowing, and intertwining. Mia felt a profound sense of recognition, a deep, intuitive understanding. These were the **blueprints**. The very language of creation.

"These are the weaves," Mia breathed, her voice hushed with awe, her needles vibrating in sync with the patterns. "The fundamental patterns of Solara's magic. The blueprints of the loom itself."

Ethan, though his instruments were useless, felt the profound logic in the patterns. His engineer's mind, accustomed to complex schematics, recognized the underlying order, the intricate design. "It's like a cosmic circuit board," he murmured, his eyes tracing the glowing lines. "A grand design for a magical universe. But… how do we read it? How do we interpret this?"

Elara and Thorn, too, were awestruck. "These are the teachings of the First Weavers," Elara whispered, her fingers tracing a glowing pattern on a crystalline wall. "They encoded their wisdom into the very structure of the Spires. It is a language of light, of rhythm, of harmony."

Their first trial within the Spires was one of **resonance and interpretation**. The shimmering pathways before them were not fixed; they pulsed with different frequencies, their colors shifting, their patterns subtly changing. To proceed, they had to choose the correct path, the one that resonated with the true harmony of Solara.

Mia's needles hummed, guiding her. She focused, extending her senses, trying to feel the subtle vibrations of each path. She felt the intricate dance of creation and deconstruction within the Spires, the constant weaving and unraveling that was its very essence. She realized the unraveling they had witnessed outside was a corrupted version of this natural process, a deconstruction without re-integration.

She chose a path that pulsed with a steady, harmonious rhythm, its colors a vibrant, consistent emerald. As she stepped onto it, the path solidified beneath her feet, and the surrounding patterns on the walls seemed to shift, revealing new, more complex designs.

Ethan, watching her, began to understand. "It's like a magical tuning fork," he mused. "Each path has a specific frequency. You have to match it, to resonate with it, to unlock the next stage." He pulled out his journal, sketching furiously, trying to capture the patterns, to find the underlying mathematical principles.

They moved deeper into the Spires, navigating through chambers of shimmering light and glowing patterns. The challenges here were not about brute force or clever illusions, but about understanding, about attunement, about learning the language of the First Weavers.

One chamber was filled with **"Echoing Harmonies."** Here, the air vibrated with a cacophony of overlapping melodies, ancient Solaraean songs, each one beautiful on its own, but clashing in a discordant symphony. To proceed, they had to isolate the true harmony, the fundamental melody that underpinned all others.

Mia felt the overwhelming influx of sound, a dizzying swirl of conflicting frequencies that left her feeling disoriented. Her needles vibrated frantically, trying to untangle the chaotic melodies.

Elara stepped forward, her face serene despite the swirling chaos. She closed her eyes, and began to hum a soft, intricate melody, an ancient Solaraean song that seemed to resonate with the very core of the Spires. Her music was a balm against the chaos, a reminder of Solara's inherent harmony. As she hummed, the discordant melodies around them began to soften, to recede, allowing the true, underlying harmony to emerge, clear and resonant.

"The song of creation," Elara explained, her voice a gentle murmur. "It is the first melody, the one from which all others are woven. When the weave is true, its song is clear."

Mia, listening to Elara's pure melody, understood. Her needles began to hum in sync with the true harmony, guiding her. She pulled out a skein of shimmering, iridescent yarn, focusing on **clarity, purity, harmonic resonance**. She began to knit, not a physical object, but a **"Harmony Weave,"** a pattern that resonated with the true melody, amplifying it, clarifying it.

As she knitted, the iridescent yarn seemed to merge with the air, becoming one with the music. The discordant melodies in the chamber dissolved entirely, replaced by a single, pure, resonant harmony that filled the chamber with a profound sense of peace. The pathway forward, previously obscured by the chaotic sounds, now glowed with a clear, inviting light.

They moved deeper, Mia's understanding of Solara's magical architecture deepening with every trial. She was learning to perceive magic not just as energy, but as a complex, interwoven system of patterns and frequencies.

Their next trial involved **"Temporal Reflections."** Here, the crystalline walls of the Spires would shimmer, and projections of moments in Solara's history would play out before them, similar to the Memory Weaves in the maze, but far more intricate and profound. They were not just images, but full sensory experiences, pulling them into the past, forcing them to relive moments of creation, of growth, of profound change, and of the subtle beginnings of the unraveling.

Mia felt a dizzying swirl of conflicting emotions through her needles, a cacophony of past and present that left her feeling nauseous and disoriented. She witnessed the First Weavers, beings of pure light and profound wisdom, meticulously weaving Solara into existence, thread by shimmering thread. She saw the creation of the sapphire trees, the glowing flora, the melodic rivers, each element a deliberate act of weaving, imbued with specific magical properties and a unique resonance.

But then, the visions shifted. She saw the subtle introduction of a foreign element, a faint, almost imperceptible discord in the grand weave. It was not malicious, not a direct attack, but a subtle *deviation* in the pattern, a tiny flaw introduced during a period of intense cosmic flux, long before Malakor. This deviation, over eons, had slowly begun to exert a subtle pressure on the Great Weave, causing the threads to thin, to lose their cohesion, to *unravel*. Malakor's darkness had simply exploited this pre-existing vulnerability, accelerating the decay.

Mia felt a profound sense of understanding. The unraveling was not a disease; it was a **structural flaw**, a subtle imperfection in the original design, exacerbated by external forces. Her mending had failed because it was trying to fix a symptom, not the root cause. She needed to re-engineer the flaw itself.

Ethan, too, was experiencing the temporal reflections, his mind grappling with the sheer scale of the information. He saw the intricate energy flows, the complex magical equations that underpinned Solara's creation. He saw the subtle deviation, a minute shift in a foundational frequency, a tiny miscalculation in the grand design. "It's like a single line of corrupted code in a massive operating system," he murmured, his eyes wide with revelation. "It doesn't crash the system immediately, but over time, it causes instability, decay."

Thorn and Elara, steeped in Solaraean lore, recognized the ancient events, their faces filled with a mixture of sorrow and enlightenment. "The Time of Whispers," Thorn rumbled, identifying a period of subtle discord in Solaraean history. "The legends spoke of a 'faint tremor in the heart of the world,' but its cause was lost to time."

Mia, with her renewed understanding, pulled out a skein of shimmering, iridescent yarn, focusing on **re-patterning, re-calibration, fundamental correction**. She began to knit, not a physical object, but a **"Corrective Weave,"** a pattern that mirrored the original flaw, but subtly altered it, introducing a new, stabilizing frequency, a perfect counter to the inherent deviation. She was learning to *re-write* the very code of existence.

As she knitted, the iridescent yarn seemed to merge with the temporal reflections, subtly altering the past, not by changing events, but by correcting the underlying magical instability that had led to the unraveling. The visions in the chamber stabilized, becoming clearer, more harmonious, reflecting a future where the flaw was mended. The pathway forward, previously obscured by the chaotic temporal shifts, now glowed with a clear, steady light.

They moved deeper into the Spires, Mia's understanding of Solara's magical architecture growing exponentially. She was learning to perceive magic not just as energy, but as a complex, interwoven system of patterns, frequencies, and fundamental algorithms. Her needles, once tools for creation, were now instruments of profound re-engineering.

Their next trial was the **"Chamber of Unbound Threads."** Here, the air was thick with shimmering, chaotic threads of raw magic, swirling and intertwining in a dizzying maelstrom of unbound energy. These were the fundamental threads of creation, separated from their patterns, unstable and dangerous. To proceed, Mia had to re-weave them into a coherent, stable pattern.

Mia felt the overwhelming, chaotic energy, a dizzying sensation that threatened to pull her own magical essence apart. Her needles vibrated wildly, trying to grasp the elusive threads. This was pure, raw magic, untamed and unpredictable.

She closed her eyes, focusing on the fundamental principles of weaving she had learned. Every thread had a place, a purpose, a connection. She pulled out a skein of pure, vibrant gold yarn, focusing on **order, integration, fundamental pattern**. She began to knit, not a physical object, but a **"Pattern of Order,"** a complex, intricate weave that mirrored the underlying structure of the Great Weave, drawing the chaotic threads into its embrace.

As she knitted, the golden yarn seemed to expand, its threads reaching out, gently coaxing the unbound magical threads into its pattern. The chaotic maelstrom in the chamber began to settle, the swirling threads coalescing, intertwining, forming a vast, shimmering tapestry of light and energy. The air grew still, filled with a profound sense of peace and order.

Ethan, watching, was mesmerized. "It's like you're creating a magnetic field for magic!" he whispered, his eyes wide with awe. "You're literally imposing order on chaos!"

Thorn and Elara, too, watched with profound reverence. "The First Weavers understood this," Elara murmured. "That creation is not just about bringing things into being, but about bringing them into harmony, into order."

Mia, panting from the immense effort, tied off the last knot. The Chamber of Unbound Threads was now a place of serene beauty, its walls adorned with a vast, shimmering tapestry of perfectly ordered magical threads. The pathway forward, previously obscured by the chaotic energy, now glowed with a clear, inviting light.

They moved deeper into the Spires, Mia's mastery of her magic growing with every challenge. She was not just a Heart Weaver; she was becoming a **Master Weaver**, capable of understanding and manipulating the very fabric of reality.

Their final trial was the **"Core Chamber."** They emerged into a vast, circular chamber, open to the sky, where the twin moons shone with an almost blinding brilliance. In the center of the chamber, a colossal, spiraling structure of pure, crystalline light reached towards the heavens, its tendrils intertwining to form a massive, intricate **"Loom of Existence."** Its threads, shimmering with every color of the rainbow, pulsed with an immense, benevolent energy, a profound sense of ancient harmony. This was the true Heart of Solara, the very core of its being, the source of its constant weaving, the anchor of its realm.

But the Loom of Existence was not perfect. A single, massive thread, glowing with a dull, sickly grey, was slowly unraveling from its center, its fibers dissolving into nothingness. It was the source of the unraveling, the core of Solara's internal decay. And as it unraveled, the entire Loom trembled, its vibrant colors dimming, its harmonious hum faltering. This was the same unraveling thread Mia had seen in the Loom of Creation in the Verdant Maze, but here, at the very heart of Solara, its decay was far more pronounced, far more critical.

"The source," Elara whispered, her voice filled with profound sadness. "The Heart of the World itself is unraveling."

Suddenly, from the shadows of the Loom, a figure emerged. Not a creature of darkness, but a being woven from the Spires' own essence, a colossal, humanoid figure formed from intertwining crystalline light and glowing patterns. Its eyes, like polished emeralds, held an ancient wisdom, but also a profound sorrow. It was the **Prime Guardian of the Spires**, a living embodiment of the Spires' purpose, its final test.

"You have come far, Weaver," the Guardian rumbled, its voice a deep, resonant hum that vibrated through the chamber. "You have learned to weave with the maze, to understand its patterns. You have learned to mend the unraveling. But can you mend the un-mendable? Can you reweave the thread of its very being? Can you correct the fundamental flaw in the Loom of Existence?" Its gaze fixed on Mia, a silent, ancient challenge.

Mia looked at the unraveling thread, then at her needles, now humming with a profound, resonant warmth, vibrating with the boundless power of the Spires. She understood. This was the ultimate test. Not just to mend, but to reweave a foundational thread, to understand the very process of unraveling and to reverse it. This was the blueprint she had sought. The knowledge was hers. Now, she had to apply it.

"I will try," Mia declared, her voice clear and strong, resonating with a newfound confidence, a profound sense of purpose. She pulled out a skein of shimmering, iridescent yarn, the kind she had used for her Mirror Weave and her Corrective Weave, but this time, she focused on **reconstruction, re-integration, ultimate harmony, and cosmic recalibration**. She approached the Loom of Existence, her needles poised. She began to knit, not just on the unraveling thread, but on the very essence of the Loom itself, weaving a new pattern of profound stability, a blueprint for its enduring harmony, a correction to the ancient flaw.

As she knitted, the iridescent yarn seemed to merge with the Loom, becoming one with its essence. The dull, sickly grey thread began to shimmer, its fibers coalescing, re-forming, slowly re-integrating into the vibrant tapestry of the Loom. The Loom of Existence hummed with a renewed intensity, its colors brightening, its harmonious song swelling, filling the chamber with a profound sense of peace and vitality.

Mia poured every ounce of her magic, every fiber of her being, into the weaving. It was a monumental task, a profound act of creation that went beyond simple mending. She was reweaving the very fabric of existence, understanding the intricate dance of creation and deconstruction, correcting an ancient flaw that had plagued Solara for eons. The knowledge she had gained in the Spires flowed through her, guiding her hands, allowing her to understand the precise frequencies, the delicate patterns, the fundamental algorithms that governed the Loom of Existence.

Ethan, meanwhile, had found a series of ancient crystalline tablets embedded in the floor of the Core Chamber. They glowed with faint, pulsing lights, displaying complex diagrams and equations that mirrored the patterns Mia was weaving. He realized these were the First Weavers' original schematics, their blueprints for Solara. He worked furiously, his mind racing, trying to interpret the ancient data, to understand the precise nature of the cosmic imbalance.

"Mia!" Ethan yelled, his voice strained. "The data! It shows the unraveling isn't just affecting Solara! It's a **cosmic imbalance**! It's a flaw in the Great Weave itself, affecting multiple realms! Solara is just one of the first to show the symptoms!"

Mia's heart pounded. The implications were staggering. This wasn't just about saving Solara; it was about saving the entire Great Weave, perhaps even her own world. The weight of this new revelation pressed down on her, but it also ignited a fierce determination. She was not just the Heart Weaver of Solara; she was a Weaver of Worlds.

She pushed harder, channeling more magic, more will, into the Loom. The iridescent yarn pulsed with blinding light, its threads weaving with impossible speed, correcting the ancient flaw, re-integrating the unraveling thread, and reinforcing the Loom's entire structure.

The Prime Guardian of the Spires watched, its emerald eyes shining with profound understanding and a growing sense of hope. Elara and Thorn, too, watched in awe, witnessing a feat of weaving that surpassed anything in their ancient legends.

Finally, with a last, powerful surge of magic, Mia tied off the last knot. The unraveling thread was gone, completely re-integrated into the Loom of Existence. The Loom pulsed with a brilliant, blinding light, its harmony restored, its song a triumphant symphony that resonated through the entire Sunken Spires, and beyond, into the very heart of Solara. The tremors in the land ceased. The Luminous Bloom Fields, miles away, suddenly flared with renewed brilliance, their colors surging back to their full, vibrant glory.

Mia, panting, leaned back, her energy completely depleted, but a profound sense of accomplishment filling her. Her needles, though cold and lifeless, had performed the impossible. She had not just mended; she had rewoven the very fabric of existence.

The Prime Guardian of the Spires bowed its massive head, its emerald eyes shining with profound gratitude. "You have succeeded, Heart Weaver. You have learned the weave of creation. You have understood the unraveling. And you have begun to mend the Great Weave itself. The blueprints are yours. The knowledge is yours. But the task… the task is far from over."

Suddenly, the air in the Core Chamber grew cold, thick with a familiar, malevolent presence. The light from the Loom of Existence flickered, its harmonious song momentarily faltering. A low, guttural snarl echoed from the entrance to the chamber.

Mia's heart plummeted. Malakor. He was gone, vanished into nothingness. But this… this was a different kind of darkness. A primal, ancient malevolence that resonated with the very flaw she had just mended.

From the shadows, a colossal figure emerged. Not Dreadwing, but something far more ancient, far more terrifying. It was a creature of pure shadow, its form shifting and swirling like living smoke, its eyes glowing with an infernal, crimson fire. It was a **Void Beast**, a creature born from the cosmic imbalance itself, drawn to the unraveling, feeding on the decay. And it was immense, far larger and more powerful than any Shadow Hound. It radiated an aura of pure destruction, a hunger for non-being.

"It is drawn to the reweaving," the Prime Guardian rumbled, its voice filled with alarm. "The correction of the flaw… it has awakened something ancient.

Something that feeds on the unraveling. It seeks to undo your work, Weaver!"

The Void Beast roared, a sound of pure, unadulterated rage and hunger, and lunged towards the Loom of Existence, its shadowy claws reaching for the newly mended thread. Its presence alone caused the Loom to tremble, its light to dim.

Mia's needles, still cold and lifeless, offered no comfort. Her magic was utterly depleted. She had nothing left.

"Mia!" Ethan yelled, pulling her behind a crystalline pillar. He drew his small knife, a futile gesture against such a foe. Elara and Thorn stood ready, their faces grim, their weapons drawn, but they knew they were outmatched.

The Void Beast slammed into the Loom of Existence, its shadowy claws tearing at the newly mended thread. The Loom shrieked, a sound of profound pain, and the unraveling began anew, faster, more violently than before. The light in the Core Chamber flickered, threatening to extinguish entirely.

Mia watched in horror, helpless. All her work, all their efforts, threatened to be undone in a single, devastating blow. The unraveling bloom, the whispers on the wind, the tears in reality… they were all symptoms of this deeper, cosmic hunger. And now, the source of that hunger was here, threatening to consume the very heart of Solara. The blueprints were hers, the knowledge was hers, but without magic, she was powerless. The true test had just begun.

Chapter 7: The Shadow of the Void

The roar of the Void Beast was not merely a sound; it was a physical force, a wave of pure, destructive hunger that slammed into Mia, stealing her breath and rattling her very bones. Its form, a colossal, shifting mass of pure shadow, seemed to absorb the light from the Loom of Existence, plunging the Core Chamber into a chilling gloom. Its eyes, twin infernos of crimson fire, burned with an ancient, malevolent intelligence, fixed on the newly mended thread of the Loom. The air grew frigid, thick with the stench of ozone and non-being, a cold dread that seeped into Mia's soul.

The Loom of Existence, which moments ago had pulsed with brilliant, triumphant light, now shrieked, a sound of profound pain, as the Void Beast's shadowy claws tore at its rewoven core. The unraveling began anew, faster, more violently than before, the iridescent threads dissolving into nothingness with terrifying speed. The light in the Core Chamber flickered, threatening to extinguish entirely, plunging Solara's heart into an eternal abyss.

Mia watched in horror, helpless. Her needles, clutched in her trembling hands, were cold, lifeless, utterly drained. The boundless power she had felt moments ago, the profound connection to the Great

Weave, was gone, leaving behind a hollow, aching void within her. All her work, all their efforts, threatened to be undone in a single, devastating blow. The unraveling bloom, the whispers on the wind, the tears in reality—they were all symptoms of this deeper, cosmic hunger. And now, the source of that hunger was here, threatening to consume the very heart of Solara. The blueprints were hers, the knowledge was hers, but without magic, she was powerless. The true test had just begun, and she was utterly unprepared.

"Mia!" Ethan yelled, his voice strained, pulling her behind a massive crystalline pillar. He drew his small, utilitarian knife, a futile gesture against such a foe, but a testament to his unwavering courage. His face was grim, but his eyes, though wide with fear, held a fierce determination.

Elara and Thorn stood ready, their faces etched with grim resolve. Elara clutched her glowing harp, its strings now silent, its usual melodic hum replaced by a faint, desperate thrum. Thorn gripped his sapphire wood staff, its emerald tip flickering erratically, its light struggling against the encroaching darkness. They knew they were outmatched, but their loyalty to Mia and Solara was absolute. Bean, whimpering softly, pressed herself against Mia's leg, her tiny body trembling. Hopsy, the knitted rabbit, pulsed erratically, its button eyes wide with terror, its inner light dimming.

The Prime Guardian of the Spires, a colossal figure of crystalline light, roared, a sound of ancient defiance, and lunged at the Void Beast, its massive form crashing into the shadowy creature. The impact sent shockwaves through the chamber, but the Void Beast merely rippled, its shadowy form absorbing the Guardian's attack, its crimson eyes burning with renewed hunger. The Guardian shrieked, its crystalline form beginning to dissolve, its light fading as the Void Beast began to consume its essence.

"It feeds on magic!" Elara cried, her voice filled with despair. "It drains the very essence of existence!"

"We have to go!" Ethan urged, pulling Mia. "Now!"

But the Void Beast, sensing their movement, turned its colossal head, its crimson eyes fixing on them. It let out another deafening roar, a sound that seemed to tear at the fabric of reality, and lunged, its shadowy claws reaching for them.

"Scatter!" Thorn bellowed, pushing Elara forward. He then spun, his sapphire staff flaring with a desperate emerald light, and slammed it into the ground. A wall of shimmering, crystalline thorns erupted from the floor, momentarily blocking the Void Beast's path. It was a desperate, last-ditch effort, a physical barrier against a creature of pure shadow.

The Void Beast shrieked in frustration as it slammed into the thorn wall, its shadowy form rippling, trying to pass through. The crystalline thorns, imbued with Thorn's remaining magic, held firm for a precious few seconds, their light struggling against the encroaching darkness.

"Go! Go!" Thorn yelled, his voice strained, as the Void Beast began to tear through his barrier, its shadowy claws ripping through the crystalline thorns. "I will hold it!"

Mia's heart twisted. "Thorn, no!"

"We have no choice!" Ethan roared, pulling Mia and Bean towards a narrow, spiraling passage that led deeper into the Spires, a route they hadn't noticed before, hidden in the shadows. Elara, her face pale but resolute, followed closely, her harp clutched tightly to her chest.

They scrambled through the passage, the sounds of Thorn's defiant roars and the Void Beast's furious shrieks fading behind them. The passage was dark, damp, and smelled of ancient stone and the metallic tang of raw magic. They moved quickly, their boots barely disturbing the dust on the floor, driven by the desperate need for escape.

Mia felt the profound ache of powerlessness. Her needles, usually a source of comfort and strength, were cold, inert. She was a Weaver without threads, a Heart Weaver whose heart felt broken. The guilt of leaving Thorn, of being unable to help, gnawed at her.

"He bought us time," Ethan panted, supporting her as they navigated a particularly steep incline. "He knew what he was doing. We have to make it count."

They emerged into a vast, echoing chamber, its walls covered in ancient, glowing runes. But this chamber was not empty. A shimmering, translucent membrane pulsed in the center, a swirling vortex of light that beckoned them forward. It was a secondary portal, a hidden escape route from the Spires.

"The escape portal!" Elara gasped, her voice filled with relief. "The legends speak of it! A way out, should the Spires ever be breached!"

But as they approached, a low, guttural snarl echoed from the passage they had just left. The Void Beast.

It had broken through Thorn's barrier. It was coming.

"Go!" Ethan yelled, pushing Mia and Bean towards the portal. "I'll draw its attention!"

"No!" Mia cried, but Ethan was already stepping forward, his small knife glinting in the dim light, his body a defiant silhouette against the encroaching shadow.

Elara, however, acted first. She raised her harp, its strings glowing with a desperate, emerald light. She began to play, not a melody, but a single, piercing chord, a dissonant shriek that grated against the Void Beast's ethereal form. It was a sound of pure magical disruption, a desperate attempt to break the creature's focus.

The Void Beast shrieked, its shadowy form rippling, momentarily disoriented by the unexpected assault on its senses. It recoiled, its crimson eyes flickering, trying to comprehend the source of the painful sound.

"Now!" Elara yelled, her voice strained, her fingers flying across the strings, weaving a cacophony of discordant notes that assaulted the Void Beast.

Ethan grabbed Mia's hand. "Go!"

They plunged into the shimmering vortex of the escape portal, Bean scrambling behind them. The world dissolved into a kaleidoscope of light and sound, a disorienting symphony of the impossible. The scent of ancient stone and decay vanished, replaced by an aroma of damp earth and distant fields. The sounds of the Void Beast's furious roars and Elara's desperate, discordant music faded, replaced by the familiar, unsettling silence of the plains.

They landed with a soft thud on the iridescent dust of the plain outside the Sunken Spires. The air was frigid, biting, and the twin moons, high in the sky, cast long, distorted shadows. The Spires loomed behind them, their crystalline forms still pulsing with a faint, internal light, but now tinged with a subtle, unsettling tremor.

Mia gasped for breath, her body aching, her mind reeling from the sensory overload and the profound emotional trauma. Elara. Thorn. They had sacrificed themselves, buying them precious seconds, precious escape. Tears welled in her eyes, hot and stinging, blurring the desolate landscape before her. The weight of their loss, added to Bear's, was almost unbearable.

Ethan, his own face grim with sorrow, pulled her into a tight hug. "We made it, Mia. We made it out. They bought us time." His voice was thick with emotion, but his resolve was unwavering. "We have to keep going. We have to make it count."

Bean whimpered softly, nudging Mia's hand, then Ethan's, her intelligent eyes filled with a shared grief, but also a silent promise of continued loyalty. Hopsy, the knitted rabbit, pulsed erratically, its button eyes wide with terror, its tiny body vibrating with an uncontrolled tremor.

Mia looked at her rosewood needles, still cold and lifeless in her hand. Her magic was utterly depleted. She was a Heart Weaver without a heart, a weaver without threads. How could she possibly face this new, terrifying threat without her power?

"We need to move," Ethan said, his voice firm, pulling Mia gently. "The Void Beast… it will follow. It feeds on the unraveling. And the Loom of Existence… it's still unraveling. It will draw it."

They began their arduous journey across the shimmering plain, leaving the Sunken Spires behind. The vast expanse of iridescent dust stretched endlessly before them, its surface sparkling under the cold light of the twin moons. The air was still, silent, broken only by the soft crunch of their boots and the rhythmic thumping of Mia's aching heart.

Mia felt the profound ache of powerlessness. Every step was a struggle. Her mind replayed the horrifying image of the Void Beast tearing at the Loom, the desperate sacrifices of Thorn and Elara. She was supposed to be the Heart Weaver, the one who mended, who brought light. But now, she was just Mia, a girl from Earth, lost in a magical world, stripped of her power, pursued by a cosmic horror.

As they walked, the ground beneath their feet occasionally trembled with a faint, unsettling vibration. The iridescent dust would briefly dim, its sparkle fading, before returning. Mia felt these subtle tremors through her feet, a chilling reminder that the unraveling was not confined to the Spires. It was a pervasive sickness, and the Void Beast was its terrifying manifestation.

"It's like it's following the unraveling," Ethan observed, his voice grim. "The more the Loom unravels, the stronger it gets. The closer it gets."

He pulled out his battered crystalline tablet. Though useless for precise readings, it still flickered erratically, its lights dimming and surging in sync with the tremors in the ground. "It's a tracking device," he muttered. "It's tracking the decay. And it's getting closer."

They pushed on, driven by a desperate urgency. Their pace was slow, hampered by Mia's exhaustion and the pervasive sense of dread. Bean, usually so energetic, walked close to Mia's heels, her head down, her tail drooping, a silent companion in their shared sorrow and fear. Hopsy, the knitted rabbit, remained perched on Mia's shoulder, its button eyes wide and alert, its tiny body vibrating with nervous energy, sensing the danger that still lurked.

The plain seemed endless. The twin moons began their slow ascent, painting the sky in hues of deep indigo and violet. The air grew colder, and the silence was often broken by the unsettling *pop* of a vanishing sprite, or the mournful sigh of a dying patch of flora, their lights fading into nothingness. These were the symptoms of the unraveling, the subtle signs that the Void Beast was drawing closer.

Mia felt a wave of despair wash over her. How could they escape? How could they fight something that fed on the very fabric of existence? Her needles were useless. She was useless.

But then, a faint, almost imperceptible warmth spread through her hand. She looked down. Her rosewood needles, clutched in her hand, were glowing faintly, a soft, internal luminescence. The hum was back, faint but undeniable, a whisper of returning power. It was like a tiny spark in the vast darkness, a fragile promise of hope.

A surge of hope, fierce and bright, ignited within her. She was not powerless. Not yet. The Spires, even in their peril, had replenished her. The Loom, even as it unraveled, had shared its essence.

"Ethan," she whispered, her voice hoarse with exhaustion and excitement. "My needles. They're warming up. The magic… it's coming back. Slowly."

Ethan looked at her, his eyes wide with relief. "Thank the stars! What can you do?"

Mia thought quickly. They needed to move faster, to create a diversion, to buy themselves precious time. Her magic was returning, but it was not yet at its full strength. She couldn't reweave the Loom, not yet. But she could create. She could distract.

She pulled out a skein of dark, earthy brown yarn, the kind she had used for the Mire Beast. She focused on **entanglement, binding, slowing**. Her fingers, though still trembling, began to knit. She knitted a series of massive, sprawling thickets of thorny vines, imbued with rapid growth and an aggressive, binding magic.

As she finished each one, she flung it behind them.
It landed on the plain, instantly sprouting into a
dense, thorny thicket, its vines twisting and growing
with impossible speed, forming an impenetrable wall
of sharp, barbed branches that completely blocked
the path behind them. The thorns glowed faintly
with a malevolent green light, and any attempt to
touch them would result in a painful, binding grip.

They heard a furious roar from behind them. The
Void Beast. It had reached the barrier. The thicket
held, its magic resisting the creature's attempts to
tear through it.

"That should buy us some time!" Mia yelled, pushing
herself faster, a renewed sense of purpose fueling her
aching body.

They pushed on, the sounds of the Void Beast's
furious roars and the tearing of thorns fading behind
them. The plain stretched endlessly, but Mia felt a
faint, familiar resonance in the distance – the
sapphire forests. They were nearing the edge of the
uncharted territories, nearing the familiar lands of
Solara.

The journey was far from over. The Void Beast was
a relentless hunter, a creature of cosmic hunger. It
would not give up. But Mia had her magic back,
even if only partially. And she had Ethan, her

steadfast anchor. They had the knowledge of the Loom, the blueprints of existence. They knew the true nature of the unraveling, and the cosmic imbalance that plagued the Great Weave.

They were no longer just running. They were fighting. Fighting for Solara. Fighting for the Great Weave. And fighting for a chance to understand, and perhaps, to ultimately reweave, the very fabric of reality itself. The desolate plain stretched before them, leading them towards an uncertain future, but also towards the hope of a new dawn for Solara, and perhaps, for all realms. The threads of their quest, though frayed, still held, leading them onward.

Chapter 8: The Fading Light

The biting wind on the shimmering plain was a physical manifestation of their despair, a frigid, relentless force that tore at their clothes and their resolve. Behind them, the Sunken Spires loomed, their crystalline forms still pulsing with a faint, internal light, but now tinged with a subtle, unsettling tremor that resonated with the frantic thumping of Mia's own heart. The air was thick with the lingering stench of ozone and non-being, a chilling reminder of the Void Beast, a cosmic horror that now surely pursued them across this desolate expanse.

Mia gasped for breath, her lungs burning, her body aching with a profound, bone-deep exhaustion. Every muscle screamed in protest, every step was a monumental effort. Her mind, however, reeled not just from physical strain, but from the searing images burned into her memory: the Prime Guardian dissolving, its crystalline form consumed by shadow; Thorn's defiant roar as he slammed his staff, sacrificing himself to buy them precious seconds; Elara's desperate, discordant music, a final, beautiful act of defiance against the encroaching void. Their faces, etched with grim resolve and unwavering loyalty, flickered behind her eyelids, a constant, agonizing reminder of the price of their escape. The weight of their loss, added to Bear's, was a crushing burden, a hollow ache that settled deep in her soul. She was a Heart Weaver whose heart felt broken, a weaver whose threads felt irrevocably severed.

Ethan, his own face grim with sorrow, pulled her into a tight hug, his touch a small anchor in the swirling chaos of her grief. His voice was thick with emotion, a raw, guttural sound that spoke of shared pain. "We made it, Mia. We made it out. They bought us time." He pulled back slightly, his eyes, though shadowed with exhaustion and unshed tears, held a fierce, unwavering resolve. "We have to keep going. We have to make it count. For them."

Bean whimpered softly, nudging Mia's hand, then Ethan's, her intelligent eyes filled with a shared grief, a profound understanding that transcended words. She looked back at the distant, shimmering Spires, then at the desolate plain stretching before them, a silent question in her intelligent gaze. She mourned, but her loyalty, her unwavering presence, was a small, comforting balm to Mia's raw spirit. Hopsy, the knitted rabbit, perched precariously on Mia's shoulder, pulsed erratically, its button eyes wide with terror, its tiny body vibrating with an uncontrolled tremor, a miniature barometer of the pervasive fear that clung to them.

Mia looked at her rosewood needles, still clutched in her trembling hands. They were cold, lifeless, utterly drained of their warmth and their vibrant hum. She was a Weaver without threads, a Heart Weaver whose heart felt broken. How could she possibly face this new, terrifying threat, this cosmic horror that fed on the very essence of existence, without her power? The knowledge of the Loom, the blueprints of existence, were hers, yes, etched into her mind with painful clarity, but without the magical energy to wield them, they were useless. She was utterly unprepared for this new, desperate fight.

"We need to move," Ethan said, his voice firm, pulling Mia gently. His gaze swept across the plain, his engineer's mind already calculating risks, assessing their desperate situation. "The Void Beast… it will follow. It feeds on the unraveling. And the Loom of Existence… it's still unraveling. It will draw it. We are a beacon of its hunger."

They began their arduous journey across the shimmering plain, leaving the Sunken Spires behind, a fading beacon of lost hope and profound sacrifice. The vast expanse of iridescent dust stretched endlessly before them, its surface sparkling under the cold, indifferent light of the twin moons. The air was still, silent, broken only by the soft crunch of their boots and the rhythmic thumping of Mia's aching heart, a desperate drumbeat against the silence.

Mia felt the profound ache of powerlessness with every step. Her body screamed in protest, every muscle a knot of agony. Her mind replayed the horrifying image of the Void Beast tearing at the Loom, the desperate sacrifices of Thorn and Elara. She was supposed to be the Heart Weaver, the one who mended, who brought light. But now, she was just Mia, a girl from Earth, lost in a magical world, stripped of her power, pursued by a cosmic horror that threatened to consume everything she had come to love.

As they walked, the ground beneath their feet occasionally trembled with a faint, unsettling vibration. The iridescent dust would briefly dim, its sparkle fading, before returning. Mia felt these subtle tremors through her feet, a chilling reminder that the unraveling was not confined to the Spires. It was a pervasive sickness, a cosmic decay that spread across Solara, and the Void Beast was its terrifying manifestation, its hungry shadow creeping ever closer.

"It's like it's following the unraveling," Ethan observed, his voice grim, his eyes scanning the horizon for any sign of movement. "The more the Loom unravels, the stronger it gets. The closer it gets. It's a symbiotic relationship, a terrifying dance of decay and consumption."

He pulled out his battered crystalline tablet. Though useless for precise readings, it still flickered erratically, its lights dimming and surging in sync with the tremors in the ground. "It's a tracking device," he muttered, his engineer's mind trying to find logic in the inexplicable. "It's tracking the decay. And it's getting closer. The fluctuations are becoming more frequent, more intense. It's gaining on us."

They pushed on, driven by a desperate urgency that transcended their physical exhaustion. Their pace was slow, hampered by Mia's profound fatigue and the pervasive sense of dread that clung to them like a shroud. Bean, usually so energetic, walked close to Mia's heels, her head down, her tail drooping, a silent companion in their shared sorrow and fear. Hopsy, the knitted rabbit, remained perched on Mia's shoulder, its button eyes wide and alert, its tiny body vibrating with nervous energy, sensing the danger that still lurked, a constant, tiny tremor against Mia's neck.

The plain seemed endless, a vast, featureless expanse under the cold, indifferent gaze of the twin moons. The primary moon began its slow ascent, painting the sky in hues of deep indigo and violet, casting long, distorted shadows that seemed to stretch and writhe with a life of their own. The air grew colder, biting at their exposed skin, and the silence was often broken by the unsettling *pop* of a vanishing sprite, its tiny light extinguished, or the mournful sigh of a dying patch of flora, their lights fading into nothingness. These were the symptoms of the unraveling, the subtle signs that the Void Beast was drawing closer, its hungry shadow stretching across the land.

Mia felt a wave of despair wash over her, cold and suffocating. How could they escape? How could they fight something that fed on the very fabric of existence? Her needles were useless. She was useless. The knowledge of the Loom, the intricate patterns of creation, felt like a cruel joke without the power to wield them. She was a master architect trapped in a collapsing building, without tools, without strength.

But then, a faint, almost imperceptible warmth spread through her hand. She looked down. Her rosewood needles, clutched in her hand, were glowing faintly, a soft, internal luminescence, like a dying ember rekindling. The hum was back, faint but undeniable, a whisper of returning power, a fragile promise of hope in the vast darkness. It was like a tiny spark in the vast darkness, a fragile promise of hope, a defiant flicker against the encroaching void.

A surge of hope, fierce and bright, ignited within her, pushing back against the despair. She was not powerless. Not yet. The Spires, even in their peril, had replenished her. The Loom, even as it unraveled, had shared its essence, a final, desperate gift. Her connection to the Great Weave, though strained, was not severed.

"Ethan," she whispered, her voice hoarse with exhaustion and excitement, a fragile thread of sound against the vast silence. "My needles. They're warming up. The magic… it's coming back. Slowly."

Ethan looked at her, his eyes wide with relief, a flicker of hope igniting in his own weary gaze. "Thank the stars! What can you do? Anything to buy us time?"

Mia thought quickly, her mind racing, grappling with the returning magic, trying to understand its limits,

its capabilities in this dire situation. They needed to move faster, to create a diversion, to buy themselves precious time. Her magic was returning, but it was not yet at its full strength. She couldn't reweave the Loom, not yet. She couldn't fight the Void Beast directly. But she could create. She could distract. She could slow it down.

She pulled out a skein of dark, earthy brown yarn, the kind she had used for the Mire Beast, the kind that spoke of entanglement and binding. She focused on **entanglement, binding, slowing**. Her fingers, though still trembling with fatigue, began to knit, a desperate, frantic blur of motion. She knitted a series of massive, sprawling thickets of thorny vines, imbued with rapid growth and an aggressive, binding magic.

As she finished each one, she flung it behind them. It landed on the plain, instantly sprouting into a dense, thorny thicket, its vines twisting and growing with impossible speed, forming an impenetrable wall of sharp, barbed branches that completely blocked the path behind them. The thorns glowed faintly with a malevolent green light, and any attempt to touch them would result in a painful, binding grip, a testament to the aggressive nature of her desperate magic.

They heard a furious roar from behind them, a sound of pure frustration and hunger. The Void Beast. It had reached the barrier. The thicket held, its magic resisting the creature's attempts to tear through it, its thorny branches crackling with defiance.

"That should buy us some time!" Mia yelled, her voice strained, pushing herself faster, a renewed sense of purpose fueling her aching body. The thought of Thorn and Elara, of their sacrifice, spurred her onward, a silent vow to make their courage count.

They pushed on, the sounds of the Void Beast's furious roars and the tearing of thorns fading behind them, replaced by the rhythmic thumping of their own desperate footsteps. The plain stretched endlessly, but Mia felt a faint, familiar resonance in the distance — the sapphire forests. They were nearing the edge of the uncharted territories, nearing the familiar lands of Solara, a place of vibrant life and comforting magic.

The journey was far from over. The Void Beast was a relentless hunter, a creature of cosmic hunger. It would not give up. But Mia had her magic back, even if only partially. And she had Ethan, her steadfast anchor, her unwavering support. They had the knowledge of the Loom, the blueprints of existence, etched into Mia's mind. They knew the true nature of the unraveling, and the cosmic imbalance that plagued the Great Weave.

They were no longer just running. They were fighting. Fighting for Solara. Fighting for the Great Weave. And fighting for a chance to understand, and perhaps, to ultimately reweave, the very fabric of reality itself. The desolate plain stretched before them, leading them towards an uncertain future, but also towards the hope of a new dawn for Solara, and perhaps, for all realms. The threads of their quest, though frayed, still held, leading them onward.

As the hours bled into an agonizing eternity, the plain began to subtly change. The iridescent dust, once a shimmering carpet, grew thinner, revealing patches of dry, cracked earth beneath. The air, though still cold, carried a faint, earthy scent, mingled with the metallic tang of raw, untamed magic. The twin moons, now high in the sky, cast long, distorted shadows that danced and writhed with a life of their own, mirroring the growing unease in Mia's heart.

The unraveling manifested differently here, a more insidious form of decay. The very ground beneath their feet would occasionally ripple, its solid surface momentarily dissolving into a shimmering, translucent haze, revealing glimpses of a churning, chaotic void beneath. These were not the fleeting tears in reality they had seen in the canyons; these were localized zones of active non-being, pockets where existence itself was struggling to hold. Mia felt these through her needles as sharp, cold jolts, a terrifying sensation of being momentarily unmoored from reality.

Ethan, his face grim, pulled out his battered crystalline tablet. It still flickered erratically, its lights dimming and surging in sync with the tremors in the ground. "These aren't just energy fluctuations, Mia," he muttered, his voice strained. "These are localized gravitational anomalies. The very fabric of space is becoming unstable. It's like the ground is trying to swallow itself."

They had to navigate these shifting zones of non-being, their progress agonizingly slow. Mia, her needles now pulsing with a faint, steady warmth, tried to use her magic to solidify the ground, to create stable pathways across the dissolving patches. She chose a skein of thick, resilient yarn, focusing on **solidity, stability, anchoring**. She knitted small, circular pads, imbued with the power to temporarily solidify the dissolving earth.

As she finished each one, she flung it onto the shimmering, unstable ground. The pads landed with a soft *thump*, instantly solidifying the earth beneath them, creating temporary, stable stepping stones across the zones of non-being. The pads glowed faintly, their solid forms a stark contrast to the swirling chaos beneath.

"Quickly!" Mia urged, panting from the effort of maintaining the pads. "They won't last long! The unraveling is too strong here!"

They leaped from pad to pad, their feet finding solid ground where moments before there had been only void. Bean, surprisingly agile, followed Mia, her paws finding purchase on the glowing discs. Hopsy, the knitted rabbit, pulsed with a faint, inner light, its button eyes wide with excitement, its tiny body vibrating with anticipation. They made it across each unstable zone, breathless but triumphant, just as the last pad dissolved back into the shimmering, unstable earth.

The sounds of the Void Beast's pursuit were growing closer, a low, guttural snarl that vibrated through the very ground. The thorny thickets Mia had created were holding it back, but she knew they wouldn't last forever. The creature was relentless, its hunger insatiable.

"It's adapting!" Ethan yelled, glancing over his shoulder. "It's finding ways around your barriers! It's dissolving them from within!"

Mia's heart pounded. The Void Beast was not just a brute force; it was intelligent, capable of understanding and countering her magic. It was learning.

She needed a new strategy. Something to disorient it, to confuse its senses, to buy them more than just a few minutes. Her magic was returning, but slowly. She couldn't create anything on the scale of the Loom of Existence, not yet. But she could create chaos.

She pulled out a skein of shimmering, iridescent yarn, the kind she had used for her most elaborate illusions. She focused on **sensory overload, disorientation, overwhelming chaos**. Her fingers flew, a desperate blur of motion, her needles humming with a frantic energy. She knitted a flurry of tiny, glowing sprites, imbued with a chaotic, dazzling energy, and a cacophony of joyful chirps and melodic singing.

As she finished each one, she flung it behind them, scattering them across the plain. The sprites exploded into a blinding burst of light, swirling and dancing, their tiny forms flashing with every color of the rainbow. The air filled with a deafening symphony of joyful chirps, melodic singing, and the gentle rustle of unseen leaves, a dazzling, overwhelming assault on the creature's senses.

The Void Beast shrieked, a sound of pure frustration and pain. Its shadowy form rippled, momentarily disoriented by the unexpected assault on its senses. It recoiled, its crimson eyes flickering, trying to comprehend the source of the painful sound. It swiped at the air, its shadowy claws tearing through the illusory sprites, but they simply reformed, dancing around its head, chirping and singing with renewed vigor.

"Go! Go!" Mia yelled, her voice strained, pushing herself faster, a renewed sense of purpose fueling her aching body. The illusion was holding, buying them precious seconds, precious distance.

They pushed on, the sounds of the Void Beast's furious roars and the chaotic symphony of Mia's illusion fading behind them. The plain finally began to give way to a new landscape. The dry, cracked earth transitioned into soft, springy moss. The air grew warmer, thicker with the sweet scent of unseen blossoms and the familiar, comforting aroma of ancient sapphire trees.

Mia felt a profound sense of relief wash over her. The sapphire forests. They had made it. They were nearing the familiar lands of Solara, a place of vibrant life and comforting magic.

As they entered the outskirts of the forest, the melodic singing returned, a soft, soothing hum that wrapped around them like a comforting embrace. The sapphire trees, their leaves shimmering with renewed brilliance, seemed to lean in, their branches forming a guiding tunnel, filtering the twin moons' light into dappled, ethereal patterns on the forest floor.

They collapsed onto the soft moss, panting, exhausted, but alive. Mia's needles, though still warm, now held a faint, steady hum, their light glowing softly. Her magic was returning, slowly but surely, a testament to her resilience, a promise of renewed strength.

Bean, after a moment of stunned silence, began to wag her tail furiously, her whimpers replaced by excited yips as she sniffed the familiar moss and chased after a glowing beetle. Hopsy, the knitted rabbit, pulsed with a joyful light, its button eyes wide with wonder, its tiny body vibrating with excitement.

"We made it," Ethan breathed, collapsing beside her, his body aching, his face streaked with dirt and sweat, but his eyes alight with profound relief. He pulled out their last water bottle, offering it to Mia, then taking a long, grateful sip himself.

Mia leaned against him, her head resting on his shoulder, listening to the comforting hum of the forest, feeling the steady pulse of Solara's magic. The Void Beast was still out there, a cosmic horror that fed on the unraveling, but for now, they were safe. They had escaped the plain, escaped the immediate threat.

But the journey was far from over. The Void Beast was a relentless hunter, a creature of cosmic hunger. It would not give up. And the Loom of Existence, the very heart of Solara, was still unraveling, drawing the Void Beast ever closer. They had bought themselves time, but not a solution.

They needed to get back to the Royal City, back to Queen Sasha. They needed to tell her what they had learned in the Sunken Spires, the true nature of the unraveling, and the terrifying reality of the Void Beast. They had the knowledge of the Loom, the blueprints of existence, etched into Mia's mind. They knew the true nature of the unraveling, and the cosmic imbalance that plagued the Great Weave.

They were no longer just running. They were fighting. Fighting for Solara. Fighting for the Great

Weave. And fighting for a chance to understand, and perhaps, to ultimately reweave, the very fabric of reality itself. The sapphire forests stretched before them, a temporary sanctuary, but the looming threat of the Void Beast and the pervasive unraveling reminded them that their quest was far from over. The threads of their quest, though frayed, still held, leading them onward, towards an uncertain future, but also towards the hope of a new dawn for Solara, and perhaps, for all realms.

As they rested, Mia closed her eyes, trying to process everything that had happened. The loss of Thorn and Elara weighed heavily on her heart, a constant ache that mingled with her exhaustion. They had sacrificed themselves, brave and selfless, to ensure Mia and Ethan's escape. Their courage, their unwavering loyalty, would not be forgotten. She vowed to honor their memory by succeeding, by finding a way to stop the unraveling, to save Solara, and perhaps, to save the Great Weave itself.

She thought of the Prime Guardian of the Spires, its immense, crystalline form dissolving as the Void Beast consumed its essence. It had been a being of profound wisdom, a guardian of ancient knowledge. Its final words echoed in her mind: "The blueprints are yours. The knowledge is yours. But the task… the task is far from over."

The knowledge. The blueprints of the Loom of Existence. The intricate patterns of creation, the fundamental algorithms that governed the very fabric of reality. Mia had seen them, understood them, in the Core Chamber. But how could she use that knowledge without the power to wield it? Her magic was returning, yes, but it was a trickle compared to the boundless power she had felt within the Spires.

Ethan, sensing her quiet contemplation, gently squeezed her hand. "What are you thinking about?"

"The Loom," Mia whispered, her voice hoarse. "The blueprints. I understand them, Ethan. I saw how Solara was woven, how the flaw was introduced. I know how to correct it. But I don't have the power. Not enough to reweave something on that scale."

Ethan nodded, his brow furrowed in thought. "The Void Beast feeds on the unraveling. So, if we stop the unraveling, we stop the Void Beast. But to stop the unraveling, you need immense power. It's a catch-22."

"Unless," Mia said slowly, a new idea forming in her mind, a fragile spark of possibility in the vast darkness, "unless there's another source of power. Another anchor point for the Great Weave. Something that can amplify my magic, give me the strength to reweave the Loom."

Ethan's eyes widened. "Another anchor? What are you thinking?"

"The Heart Tree," Mia replied, her voice gaining strength. "In the ancient path. It replenished my magic before. It's a place of pure, concentrated Solaraean magic. What if it's more than just a source of power? What if it's another knot in the Great Weave, another anchor point?"

Ethan's engineer's mind immediately began to process the implications. "A nexus point. A place where the magical currents of Solara converge. If we could tap into that… if we could channel its energy through your needles… it might be enough. It might give you the power to reweave the Loom."

The idea was audacious, terrifying, and their only hope. The Heart Tree was deep within the sapphire forests, a journey that would take days, a journey through familiar lands, but lands that were now subtly affected by the unraveling, lands that were still vulnerable to the Void Beast's pursuit.

"We need to get to the Heart Tree," Mia declared, her voice firm, a new resolve hardening in her eyes. "It's our only chance. To stop the unraveling. To defeat the Void Beast. To save Solara."

Ethan nodded, his own resolve hardening. "Then that's our next destination. But we need to be smart about it. The Void Beast is still out there. And it's learning."

They rested for a few more hours, gathering their strength, allowing Mia's magic to return further. Hopsy, the knitted rabbit, nestled into Mia's lap, its tiny body vibrating with a comforting warmth, its button eyes fixed on Mia's face, as if offering silent encouragement. Bean, curled up at their feet, let out a soft, contented sigh.

As dawn approached, painting the sky in hues of soft pink and molten gold, they rose. The sapphire forest hummed with a renewed sense of purpose, its melodies swelling, its light growing brighter. They were still exhausted, still grieving, but a new determination fueled them.

They began their journey through the sapphire forests, heading towards the Heart Tree. The familiar beauty of the forest was a balm to their weary souls, but Mia could still feel the faint, rhythmic skips in the magic, the subtle signs of the unraveling that permeated the land. The Void Beast was still out there, its hungry shadow ever present.

But now, they had a plan. They had a destination. And Mia, the Heart Weaver, had the knowledge of the Loom, the blueprints of existence, and a growing determination to reweave the very fabric of reality, to bring harmony back to Solara, and to protect the Great Weave itself. The fading light of Solara would not be extinguished. Not if Mia had anything to say about it. The threads of their quest, though frayed, still held, leading them onward, towards a final, desperate confrontation, and the hope of a new dawn for Solara, and perhaps, for all realms.

Chapter 9: The Heart Tree's Embrace

The sapphire forest, a place of vibrant life and comforting magic, wrapped around Mia and Ethan like a desperate embrace. Its melodic singing, usually a soothing hum, now held a subtle undercurrent of distress, a faint, rhythmic skip that resonated with the frantic thumping of Mia's own heart. The sapphire trees, their leaves shimmering with renewed brilliance, seemed to lean in, their branches forming a guiding tunnel, filtering the twin moons' light into dappled, ethereal patterns on the forest floor, but even their luminescence seemed to pulse with a faint, anxious beat. The air, though warmer and thicker with the sweet scent of unseen blossoms, still carried the lingering tang of ozone and non-being, a chilling reminder of the Void Beast's relentless pursuit.

They had collapsed onto the soft moss, panting, exhausted, but alive. Mia's needles, clutched in her hand, now held a faint, steady hum, their light glowing softly, a fragile promise of returning power. Bean, after a moment of stunned silence, had begun to wag her tail furiously, her whimpers replaced by excited yips as she sniffed the familiar moss and chased after a glowing beetle, her tiny body vibrating with a renewed energy. Hopsy, the knitted rabbit, pulsed with a joyful light, its button eyes wide with wonder, its tiny body vibrating with excitement, a miniature barometer of their shared hope.

"We made it," Ethan breathed, collapsing beside her, his body aching, his face streaked with dirt and sweat, but his eyes alight with profound relief. He pulled out their last water bottle, offering it to Mia, then taking a long, grateful sip himself. The cool, pure water was a blessing, washing away some of the lingering metallic taste of the void.

Mia leaned against him, her head resting on his shoulder, listening to the comforting hum of the forest, feeling the steady pulse of Solara's magic. The Void Beast was still out there, a cosmic horror that fed on the unraveling, but for now, they were safe. They had escaped the plain, escaped the immediate threat, and found a temporary sanctuary in the familiar embrace of the sapphire forest.

But the reprieve was fleeting. The journey was far from over. The Void Beast was a relentless hunter, a creature of cosmic hunger. It would not give up. And the Loom of Existence, the very heart of Solara, was still unraveling, drawing the Void Beast ever closer, a beacon of its insatiable hunger. They had bought themselves time, but not a solution. They needed to get back to the Royal City, back to Queen

Sasha, to tell her what they had learned in the Sunken Spires, the true nature of the unraveling, and the terrifying reality of the Void Beast. They had the knowledge of the Loom, the blueprints of existence, etched into Mia's mind. They knew the true nature of the unraveling, and the cosmic imbalance that plagued the Great Weave.

They were no longer just running. They were fighting. Fighting for Solara. Fighting for the Great Weave. And fighting for a chance to understand, and perhaps, to ultimately reweave, the very fabric of reality itself. The sapphire forests stretched before them, a temporary sanctuary, but the looming threat of the Void Beast and the pervasive unraveling reminded them that their quest was far from over. The threads of their quest, though frayed, still held, leading them onward, towards an uncertain future, but also towards the hope of a new dawn for Solara, and perhaps, for all realms.

As they rested, Mia closed her eyes, trying to process everything that had happened. The loss of Thorn and Elara weighed heavily on her heart, a constant ache that mingled with her exhaustion. They had sacrificed themselves, brave and selfless, to ensure Mia and Ethan's escape. Their courage, their unwavering loyalty, would not be forgotten. She vowed to honor their memory by succeeding, by finding a way to stop the unraveling, to save Solara, and perhaps, to save the Great Weave itself. The images of their final moments, Thorn's defiant stand, Elara's desperate music, replayed in her mind, a painful, yet motivating, loop.

She thought of the Prime Guardian of the Spires, its immense, crystalline form dissolving as the Void Beast consumed its essence. It had been a being of profound wisdom, a guardian of ancient knowledge. Its final words echoed in her mind: "The blueprints are yours. The knowledge is yours. But the task… the task is far from over."

The knowledge. The blueprints of the Loom of Existence. The intricate patterns of creation, the fundamental algorithms that governed the very fabric of reality. Mia had seen them, understood them, in the Core Chamber. She knew how Solara was woven, how the flaw was introduced, and how to correct it. But how could she use that knowledge without the power to wield it? Her magic was returning, yes, but it was a trickle compared to the boundless power she had felt within the Spires. It was like having the most intricate map, but no vehicle to traverse the terrain.

Ethan, sensing her quiet contemplation, gently squeezed her hand. "What are you thinking about?"

"The Loom," Mia whispered, her voice hoarse, the words heavy with the weight of her revelation. "The blueprints. I understand them, Ethan. I saw how Solara was woven, how the flaw was introduced. I know how to correct it. But I don't have the power. Not enough to reweave something on that scale. It would take all of Solara's magic, concentrated, pure, boundless."

Ethan nodded, his brow furrowed in thought, his engineer's mind already grappling with the immense scale of the problem. "The Void Beast feeds on the unraveling. So, if we stop the unraveling, we stop the Void Beast. It's a symbiotic relationship. But to stop the unraveling, you need immense power. It's a catch-22. A vicious cycle of decay and consumption."

"Unless," Mia said slowly, a new idea forming in her mind, a fragile spark of possibility in the vast darkness, "unless there's another source of power. Another anchor point for the Great Weave. Something that can amplify my magic, give me the strength to reweave the Loom. Something that can act as a conduit, a battery for Solara's very essence."

Ethan's eyes widened, a flicker of understanding igniting in their depths. "Another anchor? What are you thinking?"

"The Heart Tree," Mia replied, her voice gaining strength, a new resolve hardening in her eyes. "In the ancient path. It replenished my magic before. It's a place of pure, concentrated Solaraean magic. What if it's more than just a source of power? What if it's another knot in the Great Weave, another anchor point? A nexus where Solara's magic converges, a place where the threads are strongest, purest?"

Ethan's engineer's mind immediately began to process the implications, connecting the dots, seeing the potential. "A nexus point. A place where the magical currents of Solara converge. If we could tap into that… if we could channel its energy through your needles… it might be enough. It might give you the power to reweave the Loom. It's a gamble, but it's the only logical next step." He looked at her, his gaze unwavering. "It's audacious. Terrifying. But it makes sense."

The idea was audacious, terrifying, and their only hope. The Heart Tree was deep within the sapphire forests, a journey that would take days, a journey through familiar lands, but lands that were now subtly affected by the unraveling, lands that were still vulnerable to the Void Beast's pursuit. They were racing against time, against a cosmic horror, and against the very decay of reality.

"We need to get to the Heart Tree," Mia declared, her voice firm, a new resolve hardening in her eyes. "It's our only chance. To stop the unraveling. To defeat the Void Beast. To save Solara. And perhaps, to save all realms connected by the Great Weave."

Ethan nodded, his own resolve hardening, a grim determination etched on his face. "Then that's our next destination. But we need to be smart about it. The Void Beast is still out there. And it's learning. It's adapting. We can't afford any more mistakes."

They rested for a few more hours, gathering their strength, allowing Mia's magic to return further. Hopsy, the knitted rabbit, nestled into Mia's lap, its tiny body vibrating with a comforting warmth, its button eyes fixed on Mia's face, as if offering silent encouragement. Bean, curled up at their feet, let out a soft, contented sigh, her presence a grounding comfort.

As dawn approached, painting the sky in hues of soft pink and molten gold, they rose. The sapphire forest hummed with a renewed sense of purpose, its melodies swelling, its light growing brighter, as if sensing their renewed determination. They were still exhausted, still grieving, but a new determination fueled them, a fierce resolve to honor the sacrifices made and to fight for the future of Solara.

They began their journey through the sapphire forests, heading towards the Heart Tree. The familiar beauty of the forest was a balm to their weary souls, its vibrant colors and melodic hum a stark contrast to the desolate plains and the chilling void they had just escaped. But even here, in the heart of Solara, Mia could still feel the faint, rhythmic skips in the magic, the subtle signs of the unraveling that permeated the land. The Void Beast was still out there, its hungry shadow ever present, a cosmic predator drawn to the decay.

Their path led them deeper into the ancient woods, where the sapphire trees grew taller, their branches intertwining to form a dense canopy that filtered the twin moons' light into dappled, ethereal patterns on the forest floor. The air was thick with the sweet scent of unseen blossoms and the earthy aroma of damp soil. The melodic singing of the forest, though still present, would occasionally falter, a brief, unsettling silence that sent a shiver down Mia's spine. These were the subtle symptoms of the unraveling, the constant reminders of the pervasive sickness that still plagued Solara.

As they walked, Mia found herself instinctively using her returning magic, not for grand creations, but for small, subtle acts of protection and navigation. She knitted tiny, almost invisible threads of light, imbued with the property of **magical detection**, and wove them into the air around them. These threads would subtly hum, or vibrate, whenever they approached a localized zone of unraveling, a patch where the magic was thinning, allowing them to skirt around the most unstable areas. It was a delicate, intricate dance, a constant negotiation with the decaying fabric of reality.

"It's like a magical sonar," Ethan observed, fascinated, as Mia guided them around a patch of shimmering moss that pulsed with an erratic, unsettling light. "You're sensing the instability before it even manifests as a physical void."

They encountered creatures affected by the unraveling, not malicious, but disoriented and distressed. A herd of the multi-limbed deer, usually graceful and serene, moved with an unsettling jerkiness, their glowing antlers flickering erratically, as if their very coordination was briefly disrupted. Mia, with her needles, would knit small, soothing patterns of **calm and stability**, imbued with a gentle, restorative magic, and project them towards the deer. The patterns would shimmer around the creatures, and their movements would smooth, their antlers would glow with a steadier light, their distress visibly lessening. It was a temporary reprieve, a small act of mending that brought a fleeting sense of peace to the afflicted creatures.

One afternoon, they came across a small, crystalline stream, its waters usually clear and vibrant, now flowing with a murky, stagnant current. The glowing flora that lined its banks were dim, their petals curled inward, their inner light struggling to shine. This was a place where the unraveling was particularly strong, a localized zone of profound decay.

Mia knelt by the stream, her heart aching for the suffering land. Her needles hummed with a desperate urgency, but she knew her usual mending techniques wouldn't hold. She needed to understand the specific nature of the unraveling here, to find the precise point where the threads had lost their cohesion.

She pulled out a skein of shimmering, almost translucent silver yarn, the kind she had used for her Mirror Weave in the Sunken Spires. She focused on **deconstruction, understanding, mirroring**. She began to knit, not a new object, but a **"Diagnostic Weave,"** a pattern that mirrored the stream's own unraveling process, allowing her to perceive the precise flaw in its magical structure.

As she knitted, the silver yarn seemed to merge with the stream's essence. The murky water shimmered, and Mia saw, with terrifying clarity, the intricate magical threads that formed its flow, slowly dissolving, fraying at their very core. It was like watching a complex piece of knitting slowly come undone, stitch by painful stitch. She saw the subtle deviation, the tiny imperfection in the original design that had, over eons, led to this decay.

"It's a fundamental flaw in its magical structure," Mia whispered, her voice tight with concentration. "The threads that hold its purifying properties are dissolving. It's like a filter that's slowly breaking down."

She then shifted her focus, pulling out a skein of pure, vibrant gold yarn, the color of Solara's purest light. She focused on **reconstruction, re-integration, fundamental correction**. She began to knit, not just on the stream, but on the very essence of its magical flow, weaving a new pattern of profound stability, a blueprint for its enduring harmony, a correction to the ancient flaw.

As she knitted, the golden yarn seemed to expand, its threads reaching out, gently coaxing the dissolving magical threads back into their pattern. The murky water began to shimmer, its colors brightening, its current gaining renewed vigor. The glowing flora on its banks unfurled, their petals pulsing with renewed brilliance. The air filled with a fresh, clean scent, like a mountain spring, and the gentle murmur of the stream returned to a melodic hum.

Mia, panting, leaned back, her energy significantly drained, but a profound sense of accomplishment filling her. Her needles, though still warm, now held a faint, steady hum, their light glowing softly. She had not just mended; she had rewoven a piece of Solara's very essence, correcting a localized flaw in its magical architecture.

"You did it, Mia!" Ethan exclaimed, his eyes wide with awe. He ran a hand through the now-clear water, feeling its vibrant energy. "You actually fixed it! Not just a temporary patch, but a permanent correction!"

This experience, though localized, was a profound breakthrough. It proved that Mia, with the knowledge gained from the Spires, could indeed re-engineer Solara's magic, correcting the fundamental flaws that led to the unraveling. It was a monumental task, but it was possible.

As they continued their journey, the forest grew denser, older. The sapphire trees became colossal, their branches reaching towards the sky like gnarled, supplicating hands. Their bark was scarred with ancient runes, and a faint, ethereal hum emanated from their roots. The air grew thick with a sense of immense, slumbering power, a feeling of timelessness, as if they were stepping back into the dawn of creation. The very ground hummed with a deep, resonant vibration, a primal pulse that Mia felt through her feet, up into her bones.

They knew they were close. The Heart Tree. The nexus of Solara's magic.

Suddenly, the ground beneath them began to tremble violently. The sapphire trees around them shrieked, their leaves dimming, their branches thrashing. The melodic singing of the forest cut out entirely, replaced by a profound, unsettling silence that pressed in on them, a vacuum of sound that made the air feel heavy and suffocating.

A low, guttural snarl echoed through the forest, a sound of immense power and insatiable hunger. The Void Beast. It had broken through Mia's last barrier. It was here.

Mia's needles, though warm, pulsed with a frantic, desperate energy. Her magic was returning, but not yet at full strength. She couldn't reweave the Loom of Existence, not yet. Not without the Heart Tree's power.

"It's gaining on us!" Ethan yelled, glancing over his shoulder. "It's close!"

They pushed themselves faster, their bodies screaming in protest, driven by a desperate urgency. The forest seemed to resist them, its ancient roots tangling their feet, its branches lashing out. The unraveling was intensifying, its presence a chilling weight that pressed down on their spirits.

Then, through a break in the dense canopy, they saw it. A colossal, ancient oak tree, its branches reaching towards the sky like a colossal, living monument. Its bark was scarred with ancient runes that glowed with a faint, internal light, and a profound, ethereal hum emanated from its roots, a sound of immense, benevolent power that resonated through the entire forest.

The Heart Tree.

It stood in a vast, hidden clearing, its presence a beacon of light and life in the encroaching gloom. The air around it pulsed with a pure, vibrant energy, a profound sense of ancient harmony that pushed back against the unraveling. The melodic singing of the forest was strongest here, a triumphant chorus that swelled around the tree, its notes clear and resonant.

"The Heart Tree!" Mia gasped, her voice filled with hope. "We made it!"

But their moment of triumph was short-lived. Just as they reached the edge of the clearing, a blinding flash of shadow erupted from the forest behind them. The Void Beast. It burst into the clearing, its colossal, shadowy form rippling with rage and hunger, its crimson eyes fixed on Mia, on her needles, on the Loom of Existence within her mind.

"It's here!" Ethan yelled, pulling Mia towards the Heart Tree. "Get to the tree, Mia! Now!"

The Void Beast roared, a sound of pure, unadulterated malevolence, and lunged towards them, its shadowy claws extended, eager to consume the Weaver and the Heart of Solara.

Mia, her heart pounding, ran towards the Heart Tree, her needles pulsing with a desperate urgency. She had to reach it. She had to tap into its power. It was their only hope.

Ethan, with a surge of protective instinct, positioned himself between Mia and the Void Beast, his small knife glinting in the dim light, a futile gesture against such a foe, but a testament to his unwavering courage. Bean, whimpering softly, darted around his feet, her tiny body trembling. Hopsy, the knitted rabbit, pulsed erratically, its button eyes wide with terror.

The Void Beast slammed into Ethan, its shadowy form rippling, trying to consume him. Ethan cried out, his body momentarily engulfed by the shadow, but he held his ground, his will a defiant spark against the encroaching void.

"Ethan!" Mia screamed, her voice filled with despair.

"Go, Mia! Go!" Ethan yelled, his voice strained, his form flickering within the Void Beast's shadow. "Tap into the tree! Reweave!"

Mia didn't hesitate. She threw herself against the massive trunk of the Heart Tree, her hands pressing against its ancient bark. Her rosewood needles flared with a brilliant, blinding light, their hum swelling into a triumphant roar. A surge of pure, vibrant energy flowed from the tree, through her hands, into her needles, and into her very being, revitalizing her, replenishing her magic to an unprecedented degree. She felt boundless power coursing through her veins, a profound connection to the Great Weave, to the very essence of creation.

Her eyes snapped open, blazing with a fierce, golden light. The blueprints of the Loom of Existence, the intricate patterns of creation, the fundamental algorithms that governed the very fabric of reality, flooded her mind with blinding clarity. She understood everything. The unraveling. The cosmic imbalance. The Void Beast. And how to stop it.

She pulled out a skein of shimmering, iridescent yarn, the kind she had used for her most elaborate transformations, the kind that spoke of re-patterning and cosmic recalibration. She focused on **reconstruction, re-integration, ultimate harmony, and cosmic recalibration**. Her fingers flew, a blur of motion, her needles humming with an almost frantic energy, drawing on the boundless power of the Heart Tree. She began to knit, not a physical object, but a **"Grand Harmony Weave,"** a pattern that mirrored the original flaw in the Loom of Existence, but subtly altered it, introducing a new, stabilizing frequency, a perfect counter to the inherent deviation. She was learning to *re-write* the very code of existence, to reweave the fabric of reality itself.

The Void Beast, sensing the surge of power from the Heart Tree, shrieked, its shadowy form recoiling from the blinding light emanating from Mia. It released Ethan, who collapsed to the ground, gasping for breath, his body momentarily drained but unharmed. The Void Beast roared again, its crimson eyes fixed on Mia, on the boundless power she now wielded. It lunged, its shadowy claws reaching for the Heart Tree, eager to consume the source of this new, terrifying power.

"No!" Mia yelled, her voice resonating with the power of the Heart Tree. She flung her knitted creation forward. It exploded in a burst of pure, blinding white light, meeting the Void Beast head-on. The two forces clashed, light against darkness, creation against destruction, in a silent, explosive struggle that filled the clearing with shimmering energy.

Mia's light, imbued with the power of re-patterning and cosmic recalibration, began to consume the Void Beast's shadow. The creature shrieked, a sound of pure agony and disbelief, as its shadowy form rippled, flickered, then began to dissolve, its malevolent energy dissipating into nothingness. Its crimson eyes, once burning with hunger, now widened with terror.

The Void Beast, a creature born from the unraveling, was being unmade, unraveled, returned to non-being by the very power it sought to consume. With a final, guttural cry that echoed through the forest, the Void Beast vanished, leaving behind only a faint, lingering scent of ozone and the profound silence of its non-existence.

The clearing filled with a brilliant, golden light, emanating from the Heart Tree and from Mia's needles. The unraveling ceased. The melodic singing of the forest swelled into a triumphant chorus, its notes clear and resonant. The sapphire trees shimmered with renewed brilliance, their leaves pulsing with vibrant vitality. The very ground hummed with a deep, resonant vibration, a profound sense of ancient harmony that permeated the entire forest, and beyond, into the very heart of Solara.

Mia, panting, leaned against the Heart Tree, her needles still glowing, their hum a steady, triumphant thrum. She had done it. She had defeated the Void Beast. She had begun to reweave the Loom of Existence, to correct the ancient flaw that plagued the Great Weave.

Ethan, slowly recovering, crawled towards her, his eyes wide with awe. "Mia… you did it. You actually did it."

Bean, yipping excitedly, darted around their feet, her tail wagging furiously. Hopsy, the knitted rabbit, pulsed with a joyful light, its button eyes wide with wonder, its tiny body vibrating with excitement.

The Heart Tree pulsed with a gentle, benevolent energy, its ancient bark warm beneath Mia's hands. She felt its profound gratitude, its silent acknowledgment of her monumental achievement. The unraveling was not yet completely mended, the cosmic imbalance was not yet fully corrected, but the primary threat, the Void Beast, was gone. And Mia now possessed the boundless power and the profound knowledge to complete the task.

The fading light of Solara would not be extinguished. Not today. Not ever. The threads of their quest, though frayed, now held firm, woven with new strength, leading them onward, towards a final, desperate confrontation, and the hope of a new dawn for Solara, and perhaps, for all realms. The Heart Tree's embrace had given them the power. Now, they would use it to reweave the universe.

Chapter 10: The Grand Tapestry of Harmony

The brilliant, golden light emanating from the Heart Tree and from Mia's needles pulsed with a triumphant, resonant hum, a beacon of pure, benevolent energy that pushed back the lingering shadows of the Void Beast. The cosmic horror, a creature born from the unraveling, had been unmade, dissolved into non-being by the very power it sought to consume. The clearing, once a battleground of light and shadow, now hummed with a profound sense of peace, its air thick with the sweet scent of unseen blossoms and the earthy aroma of damp soil.

Mia, panting, leaned against the massive trunk of the Heart Tree, her body trembling not from exhaustion, but from the sheer, exhilarating surge of power that still coursed through her veins. Her rosewood needles, still glowing with an inner luminescence, felt like extensions of her very soul, vibrating with a steady, triumphant thrum. She had done it. She had defeated the Void Beast. She had begun to reweave the Loom of Existence, to correct the ancient flaw that plagued the Great Weave.

Ethan, slowly recovering from the Void Beast's momentary engulfment, crawled towards her, his face streaked with dirt and sweat, his eyes wide with awe and profound relief. He reached out a trembling hand, grasping hers, his touch a grounding anchor in the swirling aftermath of immense magic. "Mia… you did it. You actually did it. I… I thought…" His voice trailed off, too choked with emotion to continue.

Bean, yipping excitedly, darted around their feet, her tail wagging furiously, her whimpers replaced by joyful barks as she nudged Mia's hand, then Ethan's. Hopsy, the knitted rabbit, pulsed with a joyful light, its button eyes wide with wonder, its tiny body vibrating with excitement, a miniature barometer of their shared triumph.

The Heart Tree pulsed with a gentle, benevolent energy, its ancient bark warm beneath Mia's hands. She felt its profound gratitude, its silent acknowledgment of her monumental achievement. The unraveling was not yet completely mended, the cosmic imbalance was not yet fully corrected, but the primary threat, the Void Beast, was gone. And Mia now possessed the boundless power and the profound knowledge to complete the task.

The fading light of Solara would not be extinguished. Not today. Not ever. The threads of their quest, though frayed, now held firm, woven with new strength, leading them onward, towards a final, desperate confrontation, and the hope of a new dawn for Solara, and perhaps, for all realms. The Heart Tree's embrace had given them the power. Now, they would use it to reweave the universe.

As the golden light of the Heart Tree slowly receded, settling into a steady, comforting glow, Mia felt the last vestiges of her exhaustion drain away, replaced by a profound sense of clarity and purpose. The cosmic blueprints of the Loom of Existence, etched into her mind during her time in the Sunken Spires, now felt perfectly clear, an intricate yet intuitive map to the very fabric of reality. She understood the subtle deviation, the tiny imperfection in the original design that had, over eons, led to the unraveling. She knew how to correct it.

"It's not over," Mia said, her voice clear and strong, resonating with a newfound authority. She looked at Ethan, her eyes blazing with determination. "Defeating the Void Beast was crucial, but it was a symptom, not the cause. The Loom of Existence… it's still unraveling, albeit slowly now that its primary consumer is gone. We need to reweave it. We need to correct the fundamental flaw."

Ethan nodded, his engineer's mind already whirring, grappling with the immense scale of the problem. "The Heart Tree… it's a nexus point, right? A source of pure, concentrated Solaraean magic. Can you channel enough power from it to reweave something on that scale? The Loom of Existence isn't just a part of Solara; it's the very core of its being."

"It is," Mia confirmed, her gaze fixed on the ancient tree. "The Heart Tree is an anchor point for the Great Weave, a place where Solara's magic converges, where the threads are strongest, purest. It can amplify my magic, give me the strength to reweave the Loom. The Spires gave me the knowledge, the Heart Tree gives me the power." She paused, her brow furrowed in thought. "But it's not just about raw power. It's about precision. It's about understanding the intricate patterns, the delicate frequencies. It's about re-writing the very code of existence without disrupting the entire system."

Ethan's eyes lit up. "That's where I come in. The blueprints you saw… the algorithms. I can help you visualize the energy flows, predict the ripple effects, ensure the recalibration is perfect. Think of me as your magical architect, your cosmic debugger. We'll build a grand loom, a conduit for your weave, right here, channeling the Heart Tree's power."

The idea was audacious, terrifying, and their only hope. The Heart Tree was deep within the sapphire forests, a journey that had taken days, a journey through lands subtly affected by the unraveling, lands that were still vulnerable to the Void Beast's lingering influence, even if the creature itself was gone. They were racing against time, against the very decay of reality.

"We need to get back to the Royal City," Mia declared, her voice firm. "We need Queen Sasha. This isn't just about Solara anymore. If this cosmic imbalance affects the Great Weave, then other realms, perhaps even Earth, could be at risk. We need to explain everything, to prepare for the Grand Harmony Weave."

Ethan nodded, his grim determination etched on his face. "Then that's our next destination. But we need to be smart about it. The forest is still recovering. And the unraveling, though slowed, is still present. We can't afford any more mistakes."

They rested for a few more hours, allowing Mia to fully absorb the Heart Tree's power, its ancient wisdom flowing into her, deepening her connection to the Great Weave. Hopsy, the knitted rabbit, nestled into Mia's lap, its tiny body vibrating with a comforting warmth, its button eyes fixed on Mia's face, as if offering silent encouragement. Bean, curled up at their feet, let out a soft, contented sigh, her presence a grounding comfort.

As dawn approached, painting the sky in hues of soft pink and molten gold, they rose. The sapphire forest hummed with a renewed sense of purpose, its melodies swelling, its light growing brighter, as if sensing their renewed determination. They were still exhausted from their ordeal, still grieving the loss of Thorn and Elara, but a fierce resolve fueled them, a vow to honor the sacrifices made and to fight for the future of Solara, and perhaps, for all realms.

They began their journey back through the sapphire forests, heading towards the Royal City. The familiar beauty of the forest was a balm to their weary souls, its vibrant colors and melodic hum a stark contrast to the desolate plains and the chilling void they had just escaped. And now, Mia could feel the subtle shifts in the land, the faint, rhythmic skips in the magic, not as a threat, but as a challenge, a complex problem waiting for her touch.

Their path led them deeper into the ancient woods. The sapphire trees, now pulsing with renewed vitality, seemed to lean in, their branches intertwining to form a guiding tunnel, filtering the twin moons' light into dappled, ethereal patterns on the forest floor. The air was thick with the sweet scent of unseen blossoms and the earthy aroma of damp soil. The melodic singing of the forest, though still present, would occasionally falter, a brief, unsettling silence that sent a shiver down Mia's spine. These were the subtle symptoms of the unraveling, the constant reminders of the pervasive sickness that still plagued Solara.

As they walked, Mia found herself instinctively using her amplified magic, not for grand creations, but for small, subtle acts of protection and navigation. She knitted tiny, almost invisible threads of light, imbued with the property of **magical detection**, and wove them into the air around them. These threads would subtly hum, or vibrate, whenever they approached a localized zone of unraveling, a patch where the magic was thinning, allowing them to skirt around the most unstable areas. It was a delicate, intricate dance, a constant negotiation with the decaying fabric of reality.

"It's like a magical sonar," Ethan observed, fascinated, as Mia guided them around a patch of shimmering moss that pulsed with an erratic, unsettling light. "You're sensing the instability before it even manifests as a physical void. It's incredible how precise your magic has become."

They encountered creatures affected by the unraveling, not malicious, but disoriented and distressed. A herd of the multi-limbed deer, usually graceful and serene, moved with an unsettling jerkiness, their glowing antlers flickering erratically, as if their very coordination was briefly disrupted. Mia, with her needles, would knit small, soothing patterns of **calm and stability**, imbued with a gentle, restorative magic, and project them towards the deer. The patterns would shimmer around the creatures, and their movements would smooth, their antlers would glow with a steadier light, their distress visibly lessening. It was a temporary reprieve, a small act of mending that brought a fleeting sense of peace to the afflicted creatures.

One afternoon, they came across a small, crystalline stream, its waters usually clear and vibrant, now flowing with a murky, stagnant current. The glowing flora that lined its banks were dim, their petals curled inward, their inner light struggling to shine. This was a place where the unraveling was particularly strong, a localized zone of profound decay.

Mia knelt by the stream, her heart aching for the suffering land. Her needles hummed with a desperate urgency, but now, with the Heart Tree's power coursing through her, she knew she could do more than just mend. She could correct.

She pulled out a skein of shimmering, almost translucent silver yarn, the kind she had used for her Mirror Weave in the Sunken Spires. She focused on **deconstruction, understanding, mirroring**. She began to knit, not a new object, but a **"Diagnostic Weave,"** a pattern that mirrored the stream's own unraveling process, allowing her to perceive the precise flaw in its magical structure.

As she knitted, the silver yarn seemed to merge with the stream's essence. The murky water shimmered, and Mia saw, with terrifying clarity, the intricate magical threads that formed its flow, slowly dissolving, fraying at their very core. It was like watching a complex piece of knitting slowly come undone, stitch by painful stitch. She saw the subtle deviation, the tiny imperfection in the original design that had, over eons, led to this decay.

"It's a fundamental flaw in its magical structure," Mia whispered, her voice tight with concentration. "The threads that hold its purifying properties are dissolving. It's like a filter that's slowly breaking down. But I know how to fix it."

She then shifted her focus, pulling out a skein of pure, vibrant gold yarn, the color of Solara's purest light. She focused on **reconstruction, re-integration, fundamental correction**. She began to knit, not just on the stream, but on the very essence of its magical flow, weaving a new pattern of profound stability, a blueprint for its enduring harmony, a correction to the ancient flaw.

As she knitted, the golden yarn seemed to expand, its threads reaching out, gently coaxing the dissolving magical threads back into their pattern. The murky water began to shimmer, its colors brightening, its current gaining renewed vigor. The glowing flora on its banks unfurled, their petals pulsing with renewed brilliance. The air filled with a fresh, clean scent, like a mountain spring, and the gentle murmur of the stream returned to a melodic hum.

Mia, panting, leaned back, her energy significantly drained, but a profound sense of accomplishment filling her. Her needles, though still warm, now held a faint, steady hum, their light glowing softly. She had not just mended; she had rewoven a piece of

Solara's very essence, correcting a localized flaw in its magical architecture.

"You did it, Mia!" Ethan exclaimed, his eyes wide with awe. He ran a hand through the now-clear water, feeling its vibrant energy. "You actually fixed it! Not just a temporary patch, but a permanent correction! This is incredible!"

This experience, though localized, was a profound breakthrough. It proved that Mia, with the knowledge gained from the Spires and the power amplified by the Heart Tree, could indeed re-engineer Solara's magic, correcting the fundamental flaws that led to the unraveling. It was a monumental task, but it was possible.

As they continued their journey, the forest grew less dense, the canopy thinning, allowing more of the twin moons' light to filter through. The melodic singing of the forest swelled into a joyous chorus, its notes clear and resonant, no longer punctuated by unsettling silences. The sapphire trees shimmered with unparalleled brilliance, their leaves pulsing with vibrant vitality. The air grew lighter, filled with a profound sense of peace and harmony. They were nearing the Royal City.

Finally, after days of travel, they saw it. The shimmering spires of the Royal City, glowing brightly under the twin moons, a beacon of hope and resilience. The city hummed with a vibrant energy, its streets filled with the soft murmur of Solaraean voices, the gentle clinking of chimes, and the melodic laughter of children.

As they approached the city gates, the guards, their faces etched with worry, recognized them. Their expressions immediately transformed into shouts of joy and relief. "The Weaver! The Engineer! They have returned!"

News of their arrival spread like wildfire through the city. People poured into the streets, their faces alight with hope, their voices rising in a joyous clamor. They were greeted with cheers, with embraces, with tears of relief. Mia and Ethan were carried on the shoulders of the jubilant crowd, hailed as heroes, as the saviors of Solara.

They were immediately brought before Queen Sasha in the castle's grand hall. The Queen, her face pale with worry, rushed forward, her regal composure momentarily forgotten, embracing Mia fiercely. "Weaver! You have returned! We feared the worst!" Her eyes, filled with unshed tears, scanned Mia and Ethan, searching for any sign of harm.

Mia, tears streaming down her own face, returned the embrace. "Your Majesty. We have much to tell you. And we have hope."

They spent hours recounting their journey: the Verdant Maze, the Sunken Spires, the knowledge of the Loom of Existence, the terrifying reality of the Void Beast, and its ultimate defeat. Mia explained the cosmic imbalance, the subtle flaw in the Great Weave that had led to the unraveling, and her newfound ability to correct it, amplified by the Heart Tree.

Queen Sasha listened intently, her face a mixture of awe, sorrow, and profound understanding. When Mia spoke of Thorn and Elara's sacrifices, the Queen's eyes filled with tears, and she vowed to honor their memory with a grand ceremony, their names etched into the very history of Solara.

"The Great Unraveling," Queen Sasha murmured, her voice filled with ancient wisdom. "The legends spoke of it, but its true nature was lost to time. You, Weaver, have uncovered a truth that spans realms. And you possess the power to mend it. This is a task of cosmic significance."

Mia nodded, her gaze firm. "I believe I can reweave the Loom of Existence, Your Majesty. I have the blueprints, and the Heart Tree has given me the power. But it will require all of Solara's collective will, its harmony, its light. It will be the Grand Harmony Weave."

A council was immediately called. The Solaraean elders, their faces etched with newfound understanding and a profound sense of urgency, listened as Mia and Ethan explained the full scope of the cosmic imbalance. The Luminous Bloom Fields, which had been slowly dying, were now showing signs of renewed vibrancy, a testament to Mia's localized correction in the forest, and a beacon of hope for the larger task.

"This is a task that transcends any individual," Queen Sasha declared to her people, her voice resonating through the grand hall. "The Heart Weaver, with her boundless power and profound knowledge, will undertake the Grand Harmony Weave. But she cannot do it alone. Solara must lend its light. Its harmony. Its collective will. We will channel our energy, our hope, our very essence, to amplify her magic, to reweave the fabric of our world, and to send ripples of harmony through the Great Weave itself."

Preparations for the Grand Harmony Weave began immediately. Ethan, with his unparalleled understanding of energy systems, worked tirelessly with Solaraean engineers to design a massive, intricate conduit system that would channel the collective magical energy of the Solaraean people to Mia. He envisioned a **"Grand Loom"** not of physical threads, but of pure, channeled magic, a nexus where Mia could focus her power and the collective will of Solara.

They chose the highest point of the Royal City, a vast, open plaza overlooking the entire kingdom, bathed in the constant glow of the twin moons. Solaraean artisans and engineers worked together, creating a magnificent circular platform, its surface inlaid with glowing crystalline patterns that mirrored the blueprints Mia had seen in the Spires. In the center, a towering, spiraling crystalline structure rose, designed to act as the primary conduit, drawing energy from the assembled people and channeling it to Mia.

Mia spent her time in quiet meditation, preparing herself for the monumental task. She practiced the intricate patterns of the Grand Harmony Weave, visualizing the flow of energy, the precise frequencies, the delicate recalibration of the Loom of Existence. Her needles hummed constantly, a steady, powerful thrum that resonated with the very pulse of Solara. She knew this was the culmination of her journey, the ultimate test of her power, her knowledge, and her resolve.

The day of the Grand Harmony Weave dawned, a day of immense anticipation and solemn hope. The entire Royal City, and people from across Solara, gathered in the plaza, their faces upturned, their eyes filled with a mixture of awe and determination. Queen Sasha stood at the forefront, her regal presence a symbol of Solara's unwavering spirit.

Mia, clad in simple, flowing robes woven from shimmering, iridescent yarn, stood at the center of the Grand Loom, her rosewood needles clutched in her hands, their light blazing with an inner fire. Ethan stood beside her, his hand resting on a console of glowing crystalline instruments, ready to monitor the energy flow, to act as her anchor, her scientific guide in this profound act of magic. Bean and Hopsy were nestled at their feet, their tiny bodies vibrating with anticipation.

The air was thick with a palpable energy, a collective breath held in anticipation. Queen Sasha raised her hands, and a profound silence fell over the assembled thousands.

"People of Solara!" Queen Sasha's voice resonated through the plaza, amplified by the city's inherent magic. "Today, we stand at the precipice of a new dawn. The Heart Weaver, Mia Martinez, will undertake the Grand Harmony Weave, to mend the very fabric of our world, to correct the ancient flaw that has plagued us for eons. Lend her your light! Lend her your harmony! Lend her your collective will! For Solara!"

A wave of pure, benevolent energy surged from the assembled people, flowing into the crystalline structure of the Grand Loom, channeling to Mia. She felt it, a boundless, exhilarating power coursing through her veins, amplified by the Heart Tree's essence within her. Her needles blazed with blinding light, their hum swelling into a triumphant roar that resonated through the entire city.

Mia closed her eyes, focusing all her will, all her knowledge, all her power, on the Loom of Existence. She pulled out a skein of shimmering, iridescent yarn, its fibers pulsating with pure light. She began to knit, not a physical object, but a **"Grand Harmony Weave,"** a pattern that mirrored the original flaw in the Loom of Existence, but subtly altered it, introducing a new, stabilizing frequency, a perfect counter to the inherent deviation. She was re-writing the very code of existence, reweaving the fabric of reality itself.

Her fingers flew, a blur of motion, her needles humming with an almost frantic energy. The iridescent yarn seemed to expand, its threads reaching out, not just into the Grand Loom, but beyond, into the very essence of Solara, into the Great Weave itself. She saw the Loom of Existence, in her mind's eye, its threads dissolving, its colors dimming. And then, she began to reweave.

She re-integrated the unraveling threads, coaxing them back into their pattern, binding them with a new, unbreakable stability. She corrected the subtle deviation, introducing the stabilizing frequency, a perfect counter to the ancient flaw. She reinforced the Loom's entire structure, weaving new, stronger threads of harmony and balance.

The plaza filled with a blinding, golden light, emanating from Mia and the Grand Loom. The air vibrated with a profound, resonant hum, a symphony of pure, vibrant harmony that swelled and echoed across the entire kingdom. The sapphire trees shimmered with unparalleled brilliance, their leaves pulsing with vibrant vitality. The Luminous Bloom Fields, miles away, burst into full, incandescent glow, their colors surging back to their full, vibrant glory, their melodies clear and joyous. The melodic singing of the forest swelled into a triumphant chorus, its notes clear and resonant, no longer punctuated by unsettling silences. The twin moons, high in the sky, shone with a perfect, unwavering brilliance, their light pouring down on a land reborn.

Ethan, monitoring the crystalline instruments, watched in awe as the chaotic energy fluctuations smoothed into a perfect, steady resonance. The unraveling ceased. The Loom of Existence pulsed with a brilliant, unwavering light, its harmony restored, its song a triumphant symphony that resonated through the entire Sunken Spires, and beyond, into the very heart of Solara, and out into the Great Weave itself.

Finally, with a last, powerful surge of magic, Mia tied off the last knot. The Grand Harmony Weave was complete. The unraveling thread was gone, completely re-integrated into the Loom of Existence. The Loom pulsed with a brilliant, blinding light, its harmony restored, its song a triumphant symphony that resonated through the entire Sunken Spires, and beyond, into the very heart of Solara.

Mia, panting, leaned back, her energy completely depleted, but a profound sense of accomplishment filling her. Her needles, though cold and lifeless, had performed the impossible. She had not just mended; she had rewoven the very fabric of existence.

A deafening cheer erupted from the assembled Solaraean people. They rushed forward, their faces streaming with tears of joy, embracing Mia and Ethan, hailing them as saviors, as the architects of Solara's new dawn. Queen Sasha, her eyes shining with unshed tears, knelt before Mia, her voice filled with profound gratitude.

"You have done it, Heart Weaver," Queen Sasha whispered, her voice filled with reverence. "You have mended the threads of our world, and brought harmony back to our land. Solara is free. And its song will never again falter."

The land itself seemed to respond to their joy. The vibrant colors of Solara intensified, the glowing flora pulsed with a brighter, more joyous rhythm, and the air filled with a chorus of melodic singing, a symphony of pure, vibrant life that echoed through the entire realm. The twin moons outside seemed to shine with an even greater brilliance, their light pouring down on a land reborn.

Mia and Ethan watched, overwhelmed by the sheer emotion of the moment. They had witnessed the suffering of Solara, and now, they were witnessing its rebirth, its triumphant return to harmony. It was a profound, humbling experience, a testament to the power of courage, knowledge, and an unwavering heart.

In the days that followed, Solara fully healed. The sapphire trees grew taller, their leaves shimmering with renewed brilliance, their forms perfectly aligned with the land's restored harmony. The glowing flora bloomed with vibrant intensity, their light a constant, joyful presence. The melodic singing returned to the forests, a constant symphony of joy, its notes clear and resonant. The twin moons shone brighter, their combined light illuminating a land reborn, a beacon of perfect balance in the Great Weave.

Mia and Ethan were celebrated as integral parts of Solara's future. Mia continued her work as Heart Weaver, but now with a deeper understanding of cosmic weaving. She taught the Solaraean people the principles of the Grand Harmony Weave, empowering them to maintain the land's balance, to recognize the subtle shifts, and to mend any minor unraveling that might occur. Her needles, now imbued with the essence of the Heart Tree and the knowledge of the Spires, were not just tools for mending, but instruments of continuous creation and profound harmony.

Ethan applied his engineering mind to further integrate magic and technology for Solara's benefit. He designed new, magically stable structures, created systems to monitor the Great Weave for subtle shifts, and worked with Solaraean artisans to develop new ways to channel and utilize the land's boundless magic for the betterment of all. His workshop became a hub of innovation, a place where logic and magic intertwined to build a brighter future.

The legacy of Thorn and Elara was honored with a grand ceremony, their names etched into the very history of Solara, their sacrifices remembered as integral to the kingdom's new era of peace and harmony. Their spirits, Queen Sasha explained, were woven into the very fabric of Solara, their courage and wisdom forever resonating within the land.

Mia and Ethan chose to remain in Solara, their chosen home. They had found their purpose, their place in the grand tapestry of existence. They were not just heroes, but integral parts of the world they saved, their lives interwoven with its magic, its people, and its enduring harmony.

And though they sometimes thought of Newark, of their quiet house and the familiar streets, they knew their true home was here, in Solara, a land of magic and wonder, where the threads of reality were woven by the hands of a Weaver from Texas, and where peace and happiness reigned once more. The tapestry of their lives had been rewoven, and it was more beautiful, more vibrant, than they could have ever imagined. The Great Weave, though vast and complex, now held a new, stronger knot, a beacon of harmony that would ripple through all realms, a testament to the Weaver who dared to reweave the universe. Their adventure had ended, but their journey of continuous weaving, of endless harmony, had just begun.